Falling for a Shy Cowboy

VARGAS RANCH BOOK 2

Karen Baney

desert life
media

Falling for a Shy Cowboy: Vargas Ranch Book 2
By Karen Baney

Publisher:
Desert Life Media, LLC
Gilbert, AZ 85295

www.karenbaney.com

Printed in the United States of America

ISBN 978-1-960217-10-3

With regard to the works of man,
by the word of your lips
I have avoided the ways of the violent.
My steps have held fast to your paths;
my feet have not slipped.

Psalms 17:4-5

1

DYLAN VARGAS BLINKED under the shadow of his brown cowboy hat. Six pairs of eyes stared back at him expectantly. His mouth went dry, causing his tongue to stick to the roof of it.

Where was Adan? He always talked to the guests. So Dylan wouldn't make a fool of himself.

Heat crawled up his neck and over his face. Sweat pushed from the pores of his forehead, despite the late October breeze.

The petite redhead cleared her throat. "We're here for our trail ride." She had already said so once.

Dylan silently nodded in response. The cloying floral scent of her perfume mixed with the smell of hay and horses nearly causing his eyes to water. Any minute now, Adan should arrive and rescue him from the annoyed group of ladies. He hoped.

A frown creased the middle-aged woman's features as she dropped her hip lower and propped a hand on the other, long slender fingers drumming on her waist.

He pulled his phone from his shirt pocket, hoping to find a text from Adan saying he was on his way. Instead, he found nothing.

"You are our trail guide, right?"

Dylan shook his head.

"N-n-no." His face contorted with the effort to speak. He swallowed the tightness in his throat as heat crept up his neck and burned his cheeks almost as hot as a sunburn. He never failed to embarrass himself thoroughly when face to face with a woman. The old stutter, usually controlled, became pronounced when he was nervous and women made him insanely nervous. It's why Adan handled the trail ride guests while Dylan listened.

"I." He swallowed again. "N-n-need to kn-kn-know."

The redhead's eyebrow arched so high on her forehead he thought it might disappear into her hairline. Her booted foot tapped a staccato rhythm on the hard, packed dirt.

"Your experience."

There. He had finally said the broken sentence.

As the women conferred, Dylan's older brother's truck screeched to a halt, causing a billow of dust to rise in the air, gravel crunching under the tires. Dalton shoved his door open and stalked toward him, eyes narrowed. His loyal Staffordshire terrier, Ginger, followed close behind with her big grin. At least someone was happy.

Where was Adan?

Dalton's expression softened as he turned his attention to the women. "Good morning, ladies. I'm Dalton Vargas. Can you tell me if you have ridden before?"

Dylan's phone buzzed in his pocket. He slid it out and saw the message from his cousin Renata, the resort manager. His shoulders bunched tighter as he read it. *Adan running late. Dalton on his way.*

Yeah. Figured that out already.

He turned his attention back to the group of women. The redhead and two others had never ridden a horse before. He studied them and mentally picked the perfect horse for each. Pansy, a gentle white mare, for the redhead. Then Dottie and Caramel for the other two. The blond with short, wispy hair used to own a horse. He would give her Red, a strong bay gelding. The youngest woman in the group, possibly the daughter of one of the others, knew how to ride, but hadn't in a while. Sunflower would be perfect for her.

The sixth woman, with a kind smile, rode a few times a year. She could handle Mocha, a brown gelding with a little spunk, or Frappe, a dappled gray mare. Dylan's eyes traveled the length of her. Yeah, Frappe would be the better choice.

When Dalton launched into small talk, Dylan turned on his heel back to the safety of the stables. He swung by his office for a swig of water, soothing his parched mouth, before he started readying the horses.

"Sorry," a breathless Adan joined him a minute later with Parker Quaid in tow.

"W-w-where were you?" Dylan choked out, clearly still agitated, judging by his stutter.

Adan grimaced, apologetically. "Sorry, Dyl. I had to help... Someone with something. You doing okay?"

Dylan nodded. His stutter was old news to Adan, his best friend since grade school. Adan knew everything about him, including how embarrassed his speech impediment made him. And how it came to the surface when speaking to women.

Adan squeezed his shoulder. "Won't happen again. Promise."

"I've got. Frappe, Red, and Dottie. Can you. Get. Pansy, Caramel, and Sunflower?" Dylan puffed his cheeks and blew out a breath, thankful the stutter had diminished, even though his words were still choppy.

"Sure thing, boss."

Parker headed toward Sunflower's stall while Adan hurried to retrieve the other two.

As Dylan saddled the second horse, Dalton came into the alleyway. Dylan bit the inside of his lip, ready for the scolding.

"We need to talk," Dalton started.

It was the first time since last Saturday that his older brother looked less than pleased. Dylan really wished Dalton and his wife would have taken their honeymoon right away instead of waiting until next summer. Then maybe the coming reprimand would have been delayed.

Dylan nodded toward the saddle he had set out for the third horse. Dalton grabbed it and settled it on Red's back.

"With you taking on more responsibility managing the stables, I really need you to work on the customer service aspect of your job."

A knife sliced through him. Dalton knew how hard he worked to overcome his speech impediment and how he couldn't always control it. His brother's words hurt, even if they were true.

"I've been looking into specialists and I found someone I think can help you."

Dylan's eyes widened. "I don't know."

"She specializes—"

"She?" Dylan's mouth felt drier than the desert at high noon.

"Yes. She's a grandmotherly figure, and she works with some tough cases. Her name is Shirley Willis. She is a speech pathologist and a voice coach. She used to work with actors in Hollywood, but retired to Wickenburg a few years ago."

Dylan's shoulders sagged. The last thing he needed was a female speech pathologist. After Dalton cinched the last strap, he squeezed Dylan's shoulder.

"Trust me, I know how hard this is for you. She'll help. I think this is the only thing holding you back."

Dylan worked his jaw. "Do I have a choice?"

"You always have a choice. Though, Papi and I agree about this. It's time to try something new. See if it helps. If it doesn't, then I promise I won't ask again."

"You talked to Papi?" The ache in his chest deepened.

Dalton nodded.

Dylan let out a loud breath. With their semi-retired father involved, he really didn't have a choice. "Okay. Send me her info."

Dalton whipped out his phone and tapped several times

before Dylan's phone chimed. Then Dalton pocketed his phone and led Red out of the stables. Dylan followed behind with the other two horses. Adan already helped three of the women mount their horses. Dylan and Dalton assisted the remaining three before Adan climbed onto his own horse.

"See you in a few hours," Adan winked at him as he nudged his horse forward.

"Hours?" The redhead groaned.

Adan's laughter floated in the air as Dylan stalked back to his office, shaking his head. The trail ride was only one hour, but Adan loved teasing their guests.

As he eased into his office chair, Dylan stared at Shirley Willis's contact info for a few minutes.

Lord, can she really help me get past this?

Silence.

He swallowed down a lump forming in his throat, afraid to hope.

At thirty-one years old, he had struggled most of his life to overcome the stuttering. In school, the principal wrangled him into speech therapy classes. They helped some, but the fear of ridicule still locked him up, like this morning.

Before he could second guess himself any longer, and knowing Papi expected him to try, Dylan punched the contact. On the second ring, Shirley answered. Dalton had pegged her. She sounded exactly like his late-grandmother Elena, instantly putting him at ease. The conversation took longer than he expected. She asked many questions about his background, techniques he had been taught, and then she finally scheduled the first session on Tuesday afternoon. She even agreed to come to the ranch, saving him an hour round-trip of travel time. Maybe working with Shirley wouldn't be a bad thing.

His phone pinged a minute after he finished the call. Renata needed his help in the resort office, so he found Parker Quaid, a cowboy that helped in the stables part-time. He let Parker know where he was off to before he climbed into his truck and drove to the office.

When he neared, a blond woman buckled a child into the back seat of an old Rav. Then she pushed a wheelchair around to the back. After collapsing it, she laid it in the trunk. Something about her seemed familiar, but she never turned his way. By the time he parked, she had already backed out and driven away.

His heart squeezed tight. She reminded him of Brisa Franco. Beautiful brown-haired, blue-eyed Brisa. The love of his life. Secret love. Or silly high school crush.

Stupid. He hadn't seen her in almost a decade. Besides, the odds stacked against him. His heart belonged to a woman completely off limits — Adan's younger sister. She could be married for all he knew. Adan never talked about her. Best Dylan could tell, she had no contact with her family.

He sighed, shrugging off the thoughts as he climbed out of his truck and headed into the office to help Renata. Though, a tiny part of his heart hoped that the mystery woman had been Brisa.

"Sis!"

BRISA SMILED at the jovial greeting from her older brother as she wheeled her son Braden into the coffee shop at Vargas Guest Ranch & Resort, just outside of her hometown of Wickenburg, Arizona.

"Adan."

Her brother's muscular arms engulfed her in a hug for a few seconds before he released her. Crouching in front of Braden, he lightly tapped a curled knuckle on his nephew's chin.

"Hey there, cowpoke."

"Uncle Adan." Braden giggled. His laughter always warm-ed her heart.

"Let's say we get you some breakfast."

When Adan's hands hovered over the wheelchair handle, Brisa finally wrested the words from her emotion-clogged throat. It was harder than she expected to ask him for help.

"Thanks so much for watching him."

"No problem. Tell Renata I'm gonna be late for the trail ride."

"Will do."

"Good luck."

Brisa let out a steadying breath. "Thanks for letting me know about the job."

He winked and wheeled Braden to the counter. "Wanna split a muffin?"

Braden's bright blue eyes lit with surprise as his head pumped up and down.

Thank you, Lord, for my family.

She turned from the precious scene and headed toward the resort office. Just outside of the doors, she squared her shoulders and pasted on a welcoming smile. Then she pushed the heavy glass door open. The smell of cinnamon and vanilla calmed her.

The reception room had changed since her last visit, nearly ten years ago. Soft, classic country music played through the overhead speakers. Clusters of leather chairs created a cozy feel, next to wrought iron lamps with cream-colored shades. The warm glow beckoned her in. The light wood-looking tile on the floor gave a modern touch to the otherwise rustic space.

"Brisa!" Renata greeted her as she stepped into the room from the hallway. "I'm so glad you're back in town. I'll admit, when I saw your resume, I was surprised."

"That I wanted to work here?"

"That you became a massage therapist. I did not know. Adan hasn't mentioned you in a while."

Brisa's eyes darted to the floor. She hadn't exactly kept

in touch with her family for the past few years. A narcissistic boyfriend had a way of destroying family relationships. She shook off the memories. She was free now. Her life was her own again.

"Yeah, I worked at one of the big chain places for a few years after getting certified. But I missed home and am back now." For good, she hoped.

More than home, she missed feeling safe. Missed the small town life. The city wasn't for her. She had gotten it out of her system.

Now that Braden... She pushed that thought away, too. She must focus on her interview, not break down over circumstances she could not control.

"Speaking of Adan, he said to tell you he would be late for the trail ride."

Renata's smile faded, and she grabbed her phone from her back pocket. While biting her lower lip, her thumbs flew across the screen before she looked up again.

"Sorry about that. Come on in. Want some water?"

Brisa accepted the water bottle and followed Renata into her office. A large dark wood desk sat in the middle of a room lined with file cabinets. A mini fridge hid behind the desk. One wall held a map of the thirty-five thousand acres of the ranch and resort property, including a few areas flagged for construction.

When Renata's phone chimed, she begged Brisa's pardon, tapped out another message, then set her phone on her desk.

Brisa retrieved a copy of her resume from her purse and handed it to Renata. She had grown up while Brisa was away. Of course, the last time Brisa had seen her, Rennie had been in the eighth grade. She had matured into a beautiful woman, full of confidence.

"We expanded the spa over the summer, hoping to hire a second massage therapist. It has been difficult to convince anyone to move to a small town from Phoenix," Renata explained. "When Adan told me you were interested in the job and qualified, I thought you might be who we need."

Brisa's cheeks warmed. "I'm glad to be back in the area. If things work out, I hope to find a place in Forepaugh. Less of a drive."

Of course, that was only if she could find something cheap enough that she could make it wheelchair accessible. She had no expectation of finding a place already converted. At four-years-old, Braden was still light enough she could carry him up a few stairs if need be. She would figure it out.

"That's wonderful. Many of the employees with families live there instead of Wickenburg."

Renata turned the conversation to her qualifications. Then she asked several questions about how she worked as part of a team. The interview lasted about forty minutes before Renata offered her the job. Brisa sent up a prayer of gratitude.

"You mentioned in the ad that there is daycare available on site?" she asked.

Renata's eyes rounded, but she quickly recovered. "Yes."

"Good. My son, Braden, is four. How do I enroll him?"

"I'll text you the link to the forms and you can fill them out online. Just include your husband's name on the form, if he'll be picking up your son."

"I don't have a husband," Brisa said flatly, annoyed by the reminder of how far she had fallen.

Renata's cheeks reddened. "I'm so sorry. I shouldn't have assumed."

"No worries. I've been gone for several years. My son came as a surprise to my family as well."

Renata cleared her throat and stood. "Do you have time for a tour, or do you want to wait until next week?"

"Next week is fine. I need to head back home."

"Alright. See you on Monday."

Brisa stood and followed Renata out to the lobby.

"Glad you're home," Renata added before she wished Brisa a good weekend.

Brisa let out a long breath. She shouldn't be upset that no one expected her to come back with a little boy. Or one in a wheelchair. If anyone suggested to her in high school she would shack up with a man she wasn't married to, she would have laughed at them. No one fathomed her as a rebel. Not even herself.

Never mind all that. It was in the past. God forgave her. Though she was still working on forgiving herself. At least her parents and brother had welcomed her back with open arms, despite their hurt feelings.

And she didn't have to worry about Braden's dad coming after them. God had been merciful in that. Something she prayed she would never take for granted again.

Brisa pushed open the doors to the dining hall and spotted Adan and Braden at a small table near the coffee shop. As she walked toward them, Braden's eyes lit up.

"Mommy!" Braden's glee warmed her heart. It quickly faded to sorrow as he squirmed in his wheelchair. She hurried toward him and scooped him into a big hug, since he could no longer run to her. As she breathed in the fruity scent of his shampoo, a tear squeezed from the corner of her eye.

Adan rested a hand on Braden's head. "See you later, squirt."

Then his blue eyes locked on hers, one eyebrow raised. "Did you get the job?"

"Yeah. I start Monday."

"Good. I gotta run, but we'll talk later."

"Thanks again."

As Adan rushed out the door, Brisa thanked God for the hundredth time for His mercy and love and the love of her family—none of which she deserved. Then she placed Braden back in his chair.

Drake Vargas introduced himself and greeted her with a

smile as he ambled toward the table. She barely recognized him. He was just a middle schooler when she graduated from high school. Good grief, he had facial hair now.

"Welcome back. Can I get you anything?"

Brisa bit her lower lip. She could afford a small treat. "Iced cinnamon latte."

"Coming right up."

She yanked a card from her wallet, but Drake refused to take it.

"On the house today."

She doubted that. More than likely, Adan had told him he would pay for anything she wanted. She thanked Drake anyway.

While she waited, she watched her son. Braden's eyes drooped and his teddy bear listed to the side, wedged between the stump of his leg and the side of his wheelchair. A sob caught in her throat, and she swallowed hard to force it down.

If only she had left Tristin sooner. Maybe her son would still have his legs. Her failures cost him a normal future. It wasn't fair that Braden had to pay for her mistakes.

An outsider might consider Braden a mistake, too. He wasn't. Despite being an unplanned baby, Braden had been the greatest blessing in her life. A light in the darkness. A promise of something good to come from the brutality she had endured at Tristin's hands.

A flash from her right startled her and she ducked, reflexes born from a life with Tristin.

"I'm sorry," Drake's gentle voice said. "I didn't mean to scare you."

"I was deep in thought and didn't hear you." She tried to explain away her bizarre reaction.

Drake set the coffee in front of her before he scurried back to the counter to help another guest.

Brisa sipped the cool beverage as her eyes scanned the dining hall. A fresh coat of distressed paint covered the walls. Turquoise, orange, yellow, and rust decor brought a southwestern flair to the space.

A large row of folding glass doors lined one wall. She had seen similar ones in the resort dining rooms near her old apartment. In the cooler, eighty-degree fall days like today, the doors folded to the side, allowing the room to blend seamlessly with the beautiful outdoors.

Dalton Peak stood tall and proud, much like the generations of men who bore the name. Brilliant blue skies complemented the rust and gold tones of the mountain.

Brisa glanced at the neatly stenciled family motto over the main doors.

I do not dV8 from the Lord's plan.

A smile stretched across her lips as she remembered the dual meaning of the family's brand. A lowercase "d" for the first name of all the boys. Uppercase "V" for Vargas. When combined with the "8", it completed the word "deviate" in the family motto.

The Vargas family truly lived it out. She remembered many times when her father, and Dalton Vargas the third, Drake's father, had helped repair a family's house. Her mother and Catalina Vargas often had organized a meal train for grieving or needy families in their community.

That was small-town Arizona to her. Neighbor helping neighbor simply because it was the right thing to do.

Brisa finished her latte and cleared the table. Then she wheeled her sleeping son out to her silver Rav. After he settled in his booster seat, she stowed his chair in the trunk and drove home, grateful for the opportunity to start over in a safe place.

2

TUESDAY MORNING, DYLAN sent up an extra prayer for his session with Shirley. She had texted to confirm the address and time. His stomach soured the more he thought about the upcoming session. If Dalton hadn't pressed him on it, he wouldn't be trying to "fix" his stutter.

He still wasn't sure it was possible. It's not like he hadn't tried before. Many times. A speech pathologist in middle school. A counselor in high school when they thought the symptoms came from his state of mind. Many, many prayers of his family over the years. Even his own prayers from time to time. One thing he knew for certain, God had no plans to cure him miraculously.

For you, O Lord, are my hope, my trust, O Lord, from my youth.

Dylan took some comfort from the Psalm as he led Sunflower out to the corral. He ought to place his hope in God, but it was not always easy. He removed the bridle and entered the stables. After placing the bridle over Pansy's head, he walked her to the corral. Repeating the motions, he soon had all the trail horses settled in the corral with room to stretch their legs, run, and play.

Several birds chirped from a tall live oak tree nearby as a gentle breeze rustled its leaves. Pansy's whinny drew his attention to the fence line. His cousin Renata, or Rennie as they all called her, escorted a gorgeous blond toward the corral.

Rennie greeted Pansy, her favorite horse, before she called out to him.

"Dylan! Come meet our new massage therapist."

After securing the corral gate, Dylan turned. There she stood. He blinked, not trusting his eyes. The blond woman was the one who had filled his dreams, more beautiful than he remembered. Even in the loose fitted navy t-shirt and scrub-like pants, he noticed her feminine curves. Those brilliant blue eyes threatened to stop his heart.

"Hey, Dylan."

A soft smile spread across her full pink lips. She had lightened her brown hair and changed the style since high school. It suited her.

He swallowed away the dryness in his throat and tried to smile. It felt forced. Unnatural.

"B-B-Brisa." Heat warmed his face as he choked out her name. He felt the muscles in his face contract as his eyes squeezed tight for a few seconds—the worst of the worst of his stuttering tics. His heart rammed against his rib cage, pounding hard enough to escape. Could he have botched his first impression any more? Doubtful.

"Hello!" A high-pitched woman's voice called out from the alley.

As more heat settled over his neck, Dylan turned on his heel, bolting from the love of his life. He hadn't seen her in ten years. Any hope he had of winning her heart quickly plummeted as he replayed the scene. How humiliating!

"Dylan?"

A short, older woman with a friendly smile greeted him. Little creases formed along the outside corners of her eyes, much like he remembered his grandmother's smile.

He nodded, not daring to trust his words after the mortifying disaster with Brisa.

"I'm Shirley Willis."

Her light perfume and spiky blond hair didn't match the image he had conjured in his mind. Nor did the bright purple shirt tucked into her stylish jeans. She had to be around Mami's age. Maybe a few years older.

As a long breath left his lungs, he motioned toward his office. "Th-th-this way." Great. More stuttering. Maybe he should tape his mouth shut today.

"Pretty property," she said as she followed him.

Once she entered his office, he closed the door, rounding his desk toward his chair.

"Did I hear that one of those women is a massage therapist?"

Dylan nodded.

Shirley's blue eyes sparkled. "Oh! That's wonderful. I might enlist her help with your therapy."

His eyes widened, and his throat dried up. He sucked in a sharp breath and choked on it. Anyone besides Brisa would be better. There was no way he could relax around her. After a few sips of water, he finally recovered from the coughing fit.

"You alright?"

Again, he nodded instead of speaking.

"Honey, I can't do my job if you don't use your words."

Shirley's tone held a tinge of scolding as she plopped into the chair across from him. He felt like a kid getting caught sneaking one of his Mami's cinnamon and honey empanadas before supper.

"Tell me about something you love. Something that makes you calm and happy."

"H-h-horses." At least that time, the facial tics didn't accompany the word.

She grinned. "Why do you like horses?"

Dylan shrugged, causing Shirley's brows to lower. She shook her head. He resisted the temptation to roll his eyes. Then he opened his mouth, dreading his next sentence.

"I l-l-like taking c-c-care of them." He broke eye contact to stare at the corner of the room. "They listen. They don't. J-j-judge me."

"You've been dealing with this a long time, haven't you?"

"Thirty-one y-y-years."

"Would you mind if I pray before we begin?"

His eyes flicked to hers. The compassion in the older woman's gaze brought him a little peace.

"Okay."

She leaned forward, the leather chair creaking beneath her, and rested her hands palms up on the desk. He placed his in them and bowed his head.

"Lord Jesus, I ask for your wisdom and peace during our session today. Guide me. Help Dylan relax. Amen."

As soon as she released his hands, she stood and moved behind his chair.

"Now, the first thing I want to do is feel your vocal chords as you talk. I know it might feel uncomfortable. Is there a verse or poem or something you know from memory that you could recite for me?"

Dylan nodded.

"Honey, this is a safe place. You can use your words with me."

"Yes."

"Good."

Her warm fingers rested on the front of his neck. She held her other hand on his spine, palm flat between his shoulder blades.

"Tell me that verse."

"W-w-with regard t-t-to the w-w-works of man." He drew in a breath, hating the way he stumbled over the family verse. Maybe if he slowed down, it wouldn't come out so fragmented. "B-b-by the word. Of your lips. I have. Avoided the. Ways of the v-v-violent. My steps have h-h-held. Fast to your p-p-paths. M-m-my feet have not s-s-slipped."

"Psalms, right?" Shirley's sweet voice held no judgment as she massaged the sides of his neck. Her long fingers dug into the muscles of his shoulders. Then she rocked his head

16

from side to side. All of which seemed incredibly weird to him.

"Close your eyes. Picture riding your favorite horse."

When he raised an eyebrow, she gave him an encouraging pat. So he closed his eyes, leaning back in his office chair.

He saw himself riding Red at dawn. The wind of a gallop spread the horse's mane and tail behind him while cooling Dylan's face. They moved in the perfect harmony of horse and rider, the blue cloudless sky overhead. The beauty of Vargas Ranch spread out before him. He could almost smell the horse and tack leather, along with the dust of the desert.

Shirley's hands continued to work his neck and shoulders.

"Now recite the verse again."

"With regard to the works of man, b-b-by the word of your lips I have avoided the ways of the violent. M-m-my steps have held fast to your paths; my feet have not slipped."

He opened his eyes, astonished that he only stuttered twice. Dare he even hope?

Shirley crossed to the other side of his desk and took a seat. "Tell me how you think you did."

"Best ever." A grin spread across his face as his back straightened. Hope blossomed in his heart.

She smiled. "I'll come back next week, same time. Your homework is to practice reciting different verses aloud. Preferably in front of others."

He frowned, and his eyes darted to the floor. He hated speaking in front of others. Too many people had ridiculed him over the years.

"Look at me," she whispered.

He forced himself to make eye contact despite the tightening in his gut.

"You can do this. But you have to let go of your fear of being judged. I know your family cares about you. And you have some friends that do too, right?"

"Yeah."

"Practice with them. If you stutter a lot or freeze, I want you to close your eyes. Picture riding that horse. Take a few slow, deliberate breaths. Relax your shoulders. Stretch your neck from side to side and then try again."

"Slow, deliberate breaths?"

"Yes, from your diaphragm. Stand up."

When he did, she placed her hand on his belly, just below his rib cage.

"Push my hand out as you take a deep breath. Then release it through your nose."

He did so. Still weird.

"Release it slowly, like a soft breeze."

The air left his lungs through his nose.

"Excellent."

Shirley snagged her purse and announced the end of the session. Not even twenty minutes.

"Remember, loosen up. Practice your breathing." She winked at him. "And consider a neck and shoulder massage from that pretty new massage therapist."

Heat singed his face. Had she seen his reaction to Brisa and his nightmarish greeting?

"Until next week, may the Lord bless and keep you."

Shirley Willis left in a hurry, her footsteps fading away in the distance, leaving the alleyway quiet once again.

Dylan crossed the room and closed his office door. What had just happened?

BRISA WATCHED DYLAN'S hasty retreat. Still aloof. She rolled her eyes. She thought he would have outgrown that by now. Who knew why Adan was friends with him?

"Sorry," Renata said. "Guess he had an appointment."

She followed Renata back to the golf cart. The whir of the engine filled the silence as Renata drove her to the spa.

After Renata dropped her off, she tried not to worry about how Braden fared in daycare. He seemed fine yesterday. She had counted nearly twenty kids when she had dropped him off this morning. She sure hoped they would be kind to him.

Brisa flicked her wrist. Her watch flashed on. Eleven-ten. Her next appointment was at eleven-thirty. She walked down the hall to her massage room. Unlike her previous job, she didn't have to share it with another massage therapist.

"Brisa," Jody, the spa manager, said. "There's a woman who wants to speak with you."

She glanced at her watch, hoping the woman would not take too long.

A short woman with spiky blond hair greeted her with a warm smile. "You're the new massage therapist, right?"

"Yeah," she answered leerily.

"I was wondering if you could help me with one of my patients."

Brisa followed her outside. Once introductions finished, Shirley continued.

"I am working with a young man on a speech impediment. I'm a speech pathologist and voice coach," she explained. "One method I've found very effective for a case like his in the past is meditation and massage. Tell me, do you know some meditation techniques you could teach him?"

"You mean like Yoga?"

"Mmm, hmm."

"Yes, but I have to warn you, my approach comes from a Christian spiritual lens. Not eastern mysticism."

"Perfect. I've asked him to practice reciting some Bible verses from memory. So that would work well with the meditation you teach him."

Brisa held back a frown. She hadn't agreed to do anything yet.

"He might come across as shy or aloof, so I could really use your help to make him comfortable and challenge him to recite the verses aloud as part of his meditation."

"Who is your patient?" she asked, even though she had an inkling of who it was.

"Dylan Vargas."

Brisa's shoulders sagged. Of course, it was Adan's best friend. If his cold greeting said anything this morning, it was that he didn't like her. Not even a little.

"I don't know."

"The other technique that would help him is a neck and shoulder massage when he freezes up. Brisa, he's afraid of being judged, so it's important that you create a safe environment for him. If you want to help."

She let out a slow breath. She wanted to use her gifts to help others. Always had. But Dylan Vargas?

A nudge in her gut that she could only describe as from God, pushed the words from her mouth. "Okay. I'll help."

Shirley gave her a big hug. "Thank you. I know it will mean a lot to him."

Brisa stared as the older woman left, doubting Dylan would appreciate her help at all. He had always seemed distant to her. Quiet. On the outskirts. Even when he visited with her family in high school to hang out with Adan.

Shaking off the thoughts, she returned to her massage room. After she double checked her supplies, she entered the lobby. She greeted her next client, a young woman who was a guest of the resort, before she led her back to the room. She gave her usual spiel. The woman wanted a relaxing ninety-minute massage. Brisa reminded her to undress to her comfort level before closing the door behind her.

She waited a few minutes before she knocked on the door. Once the woman answered, Brisa entered, lowered the lights, and adjusted the music volume.

Then she worked on the woman. Her mind wandered as

she massaged the woman's back. The music reminded her of a Japanese garden in the spring. She pictured cherry blossoms visible through a window on a shaded bamboo porch. Her hands kneaded knots out of the woman's muscles. In a few places, she leaned in with her forearm to loosen a tense muscle.

The familiar pace of a ninety-minute massage banished her anxiety. It felt good to use her talents to help others. The calm environment helped her forget about her messed up life for a few minutes.

As the massage wound down, Brisa ended with gentle circular motions at the woman's temple. She spoke in a whisper, making sure her client was awake. Then she left the room so the woman could change.

After a few minutes, she noticed the door opened a crack. She offered a recap of the session along with cold water in a disposable cup before leading her out to the lobby. Then she went back to the room to change the sheets before taking her break.

Brisa walked toward the dining hall, hoping to pick up a sandwich, even though they may have stopped serving lunch for the day. The cool October breeze felt soothing against her neck and arms.

"Bri!" Adan caught up to her. "How's it going?"

"Good. Everyone is really nice."

Adan laughed. "You've known most of them for years."

"Everyone at the spa is new to me. But friendly."

"Glad to hear it. You headed over for lunch?"

"Yeah."

"Us too."

It was then she noticed Dylan keeping pace on the other side of Adan. When she smiled at him, he jerked his gaze away. She let a soft sigh slip out, wondering just what Adan saw in his best friend. Seemed like he never said a word.

A distant memory came to mind. Boys taunting Dylan in high school. Why?

Shame slammed into her heart. She had forgotten how bad his stutter had been back then. Silly that this morning's interaction hadn't reminded her. She was guilty for judging him, too. Why did Shirley pick her to help?

When they reached the dining hall, Dylan jogged ahead and held the door open for her and Adan. She thanked him, truly appreciating his kindness.

"Hey guys, Brisa," Drake greeted them. "Got a few bagged lunches left. You want roast beef or turkey?"

"Turkey," she answered at the same time as Dylan.

Drake cringed. "Sorry, only one turkey."

"Oh, you can have it, Dylan."

He shook his head and snatched one of the other bags from the counter before darting out of the dining hall.

"What's with him?" she asked Adan, as they sat at a nearby table.

"He gets nervous around women."

"All women?" Her stomach squeezed tight. How was she supposed to help if her presence made the guy an uptight wreck?

Adan looked up and to the right as he chewed. "Yeah, I think so."

"Even his mother?"

"Probably not. But most every other woman."

She snorted.

Before she ate a bite of her sandwich, she asked her brother about his job. He regaled her with many stories while they ate. She glanced at her watch again.

"I want to check on Braden."

"He's fine. I checked on him around noon."

"Aw. Thanks."

When Adan stood to leave, Brisa stopped him.

"Can you ask Dylan to meet me tomorrow at eight? His speech therapist wants me to teach him meditation."

Adan's eyebrows shot to the sky.

"Tell him to wear loose fitted clothing, like he would to

a gym."

Adan snorted. "None of us go to the gym. We get our workout by living on a ranch."

Brisa snickered. "I'm sure he has some athletic shorts and a t-shirt."

"I'll tell him."

She thanked him and headed to the daycare room to spy on her son. She watched from the window in the door, her heart warming. Braden sat on the floor with the other boys his age. They smiled and laughed as they built some extensive structure with legos.

Brisa quickly moved away from the window before he saw her. He seemed fine. Adjusting well. Maybe she would feel comfortable in a few weeks, too.

3

"HEY, BRISA SAYS to meet her by the dining hall at eight tomorrow morning."

Dylan wanted to throw up. "Why?"

"Shirley asked her to teach you meditation."

He frowned and whipped out his phone, shooting a text off to his odd speech therapist. Her one-word reply explained nothing. *Go.*

Dylan growled.

"It'll be fine," Adan said. "It's just Bri. She's as harmless as they come. Just think of her like Rennie."

His face heated, betraying the thoughts running through his mind. He could never think of Brisa like his cousin. Hopefully, Adan couldn't read his mind.

"D-d-did she say. How long?"

Adan smirked. "Nope. I'm guessing it can't be more than an hour. You can shower after. I'll cover things at the stables."

Dylan flopped down on his bed, wondering how long Adan had kept the information to himself. Probably since lunch, knowing how much Dylan would hate the idea.

"She said to wear gym clothes."

Great. Seemed like he would change clothes a lot tomorrow. Jeans and a snap front shirt for the early morning care of the horses. Then a shower before meeting Brisa? He couldn't go smelling like horses and barn. He could probably skip a shower after the meditation. How much physical effort could that take?

He shut off his lamp and rolled to face the wall. What was Shirley doing to him? Pairing him up with Brisa? He had clarified that everything was worse around women.

That was probably Shirley's motive. Already he could tell the eccentric woman would continue to push him outside of his comfort zone.

Throughout the night, he listened to Derin's loud snores. His middle brother sawed logs louder than a chain saw when he laid on his back. Dylan had been half tempted to throw something at him. Except it wasn't Derin's fault sleep eluded him. It was thoughts of spending time alone with Brisa. And thoughts of the unknown.

When his alarm sounded at four-thirty, he figured he got maybe three hours of sleep. He donned an outfit, more from muscle memory than actual thought, before he filled his travel mug with coffee and drove over to the stables. Adan joined him a few minutes later.

They worked quietly until seven-fifteen. Then Dylan went back to the bunkhouse to shower, groom, and change into gym clothes. By the time he drove over to the dining hall, his shoulders ached from the anxiety.

Brisa waved when he hopped out of the truck. She wore her work uniform, the loose navy t-shirt and scrubs. Her long hair hung in two braids down her back. If she wore any makeup, he couldn't tell. She stole his breath anyway.

"I thought we could find someplace private with a view of Dalton Peak," she said as she walked toward his truck.

"'Kay."

He knew the perfect spot. One he and his brothers often drove to. It was only accessible by a high-clearance vehicle and through a locked gate to prevent guests from wandering there. When he pulled up to the gate, he left the truck running. Then he unlocked the gate and drove through. He would wait to lock it until they were done.

Once they arrived at the spot, Brisa let out a soft breath.

"It's so beautiful here. This will be perfect."

He shut off the engine and rounded the front of the truck right as she swung the door open. Pink circles bloomed on her cheeks.

"Sorry. I'm not used to..."

His heart skipped a beat as her voice faded. If she were his, he would always open doors for her and do anything to show her kindness.

But she wasn't his. Would never be his. Because she was Adan's little sister.

She thrust a green mat at him. "Here."

He took the rubbery looking mat and followed her lead. She unrolled a pink mat. Then she sat on it cross-legged, facing the sun. When she raised an eyebrow, he unfurled his mat and sat next to her, also facing the sun.

"See how I crossed my legs?"

He nodded, definitely not trusting his words around her sparkling blue eyes that he could easily fall into and drown.

"Rest your wrists on your knees, palms facing up. You can pinch your fingers together like this or leave your hands relaxed. Whatever feels most comfortable to you."

Dylan nodded and did as she asked.

"Try to relax. You look stiffer than a board."

Yeah, relax. Around her? Not happening.

"Close your eyes."

He did as she instructed. When her voice sounded closer—too close—he almost shot to his feet, save for her hands resting on his shoulders. She smelled like an ocean breeze and warm sunshine, as she kneeled behind him. His mouth went dry as her hands slowly moved along his neck. Tingles radiated from her gentle touch. It felt wrong to enjoy it so much.

"Dyl, loosen up. You won't get anything out of this if you don't relax."

He snorted.

She sighed.

"Close your eyes. Feel the warmth of God's sun on your face."

Her voice took on a soothing tone that strangely seeped through his body.

"The sun is God's bright smile for you, Dylan Vargas. Tilt your face heavenward and accept his smile."

As he dropped his head back, her fingers kneaded the tightness from his neck and shoulders.

"Breathe in."

He did so, catching a lung full of her amazing scent.

"Breathe out. As you take each breath, remember God's love."

He felt the tension seep out of his neck and shoulders as she guided him through the breathing exercises. When he no longer registered her hands on his body, he heard her breathing beside him on her mat.

"I lift my eyes up," she whispered.

"To the mountains," he responded.

"Where does my help come from?"

"It comes from the Lord. Maker of heaven and earth." The words flowed freely from his mouth, unhindered. Smooth.

"He made this beautiful mountain behind us. Breathe in His presence and peace."

Dylan did, picturing a father, much like his own, smiling with tender care oozing from his eyes. God loved him. He knew that. Never doubted it. But had he ever just sat in His presence before, letting it wash over him?

He wasn't sure how long they had sat there. He finally stirred when a warm hand rested on his forearm, sending jolts through his chest.

"Dylan? We should go."

He opened his eyes and noticed Brisa had rolled up her mat and had already stowed it in his truck. Warmth heated his face.

"Thanks," he said as he stood, quickly rolling up the borrowed mat. He handed it to her, but she refused it.

"Keep it. You'll need it for tomorrow."

As he neared the truck, this time she waited for him to open the door before she climbed into the passenger seat. She held his gaze for a few seconds, causing his heart to thrum loudly in his ears. When her eyes darted away, he closed the door and crossed to the driver's side.

For a moment there, he almost believed she felt the same thing he had. Unlikely, but a guy could hope, right?

BRISA'S BREATH LEFT in a rush after Dylan closed the passenger door. Something in his eyes had made it hard to look away. She snorted. All she had done was teach him how to meditate. They had recited scripture together.

Yet it touched a long forgotten, broken place in her heart. Dylan's weakness and willingness to accept her help humbled her. It was the same attitude she should have with her family. Quiet acceptance. After all, wasn't that why she had moved home? So they could help?

"Should I drive you straight to the spa?"

Her heart cheered him on. A complete sentence without stumbling. Maybe that Shirley lady was on to something.

"If you have time."

"Yeah."

Silence settled over the rest of their ride back. Not a strained, awkward silence like earlier. Instead, a peace had settled over both of them.

Brisa looked out the window, watching the desert landscape go by as the truck bumped and jostled over the uneven terrain, kicking up dust in its wake. Dalton Peak stood to the west. She always liked how it looked different depending on the light and time of day. Like now. The gold hues had faded and the rust and purple tones popped. The bright green trunks of the palo verde trees contrasted against the mountain backdrop. She missed this place—not that Vargas Ranch had ever been her home.

Her old life in the city nearly destroyed her and her son. Never a moment's peace. Her goal each day had been to survive and to take care of Braden. This place promised the do-over she wanted.

When Dylan pulled his truck to a stop, he shifted into park. Brisa hesitated with her fingers resting on the handle until he opened and closed his door. She knew his chivalry had nothing to do with her. Just her gender and his mother's excellent training. All the Vargas boys—er, men—treated women well. How utterly foreign to the life she had lived for the past several years.

"Same time tomorrow," she called over her shoulder as he held the spa door open for her.

"Yup."

A smile stretched across her lips at his one-word answer. She ducked her head as she hurried down the hall to her room. At the end of each day, she left everything set up for her first client the following day, so she had no work needing her attention. Still, she needed a few minutes to gather her thoughts before facing any of her co-workers or clients.

So far, she had enjoyed getting to know her co-workers. There was Jody, the spa manager. A pleasant lady around Adan's age, maybe older. From what she had learned yesterday, Jody was the only married person who worked in the spa. She had two kids, a second-grader and a five-year-old who started kindergarten this year.

Then the hairstylist, Ruth, was a single mom in her early forties. She raised her sophomore son and senior daughter alone. She mentioned she had divorced her husband, but he wasn't in the picture anymore. The way she said it left Brisa certain he was still alive.

Amber, the nail tech, reminded her of her closest friend

at her old job. Bubbly. Outgoing. Young—only twenty-five. Brisa snorted. She was only four years older than her. Though the rough life she had lived made her feel like she was thirty-five.

Christi, the other massage therapist, kept to herself. Brisa only knew her age, twenty-seven, and nothing else about her. She hoped to become friends in time.

Jody poked her head into the room. "Your first client is here."

Brisa greeted the stunning redhead who complained about soreness from her trail ride late last week. Brisa eased off the pressure when the woman whimpered while she worked on her legs. Yeah, she should expect to see a few folks with similar tenderness if they were inexperienced riders.

Even being around horses and on the ranch helped her feel more at home. It had been a wise decision to come back. Soon enough, she would find a house and get settled. She and her son would start over.

At lunch time, Brisa walked down to the dining hall, about a ten minute leisurely walk from the spa. A lovely blond woman with a welcoming smile stood when she entered.

"You must be Brisa. I'm River Sl—Vargas." She laughed as she wiggled her left hand, showing off the wedding band and engagement ring. "Still getting used to married life. I'm Dalton's wife."

"Oh, I heard you and he were married recently. No honeymoon?"

River's smile grew brighter. "We're planning a big trip to Hawaii in May."

"So long from now?"

"This time of year is too busy for Dalton. It's more important to me to have a less stressed husband than a honeymoon right away. We have our whole lives for fun trips."

Brisa found River's smile and mindset contagious.

"We also didn't want a long engagement. So... Here we are."

Brisa sat across from River and prayed over her sandwich before she started eating.

"I heard from Adan that you just moved back home with your son. Devon adores Braden already."

"Aw. That's good to learn. It surprised me to hear Devon is working with the kids."

"He's filling in until we hire a children's program director." River lowered her voice. "Though, I secretly wonder if he's dragging his feet hiring because he loves the kids so much."

River sipped her mocha as Brisa felt the scrutiny of her gaze.

"Has anyone invited you to our Thursday morning Bible study yet?"

Brisa shook her head.

"Oh, you must come. It's a women's only study. Me, Catalina, Renata, Solana, Jody, Ruth, and Amber get together from nine to ten-thirty. We already block everyone's calendar, so we make no appointments."

"Um. Are you sure?"

"Of course. You'll never guess who covers the front office while we meet."

Brisa raised an eyebrow.

"Your brother."

"Really?" That tidbit surprised her.

"He said he thinks it's important for all the amazing women in his life to take time for themselves."

"My brother, Adan?"

River nodded emphatically. "I know, right?"

"Huh."

"He even started a study for the men on Tuesday evenings. At the bunkhouse. Dalton, his father, and grandfather all attend too."

"Wow." In the time she had been gone, Adan had

changed a lot. More than she realized. He seemed more serious than ever about his faith. The least she could do was follow his example.

"Where do we meet?"

"In the private room off the dining hall."

"Thanks. Should I bring anything?"

"Just yourself, your Bible, and a notebook."

Brisa felt a little lighter at the prospect of connecting with other women. Maybe Mom would come too.

The next morning, Brisa asked Dylan to drop her off at the dining hall once they completed their meditation. She was proud of the way he had embraced the practice. He even recited a few verses from Psalm 34 flawlessly.

She waved to him as he backed out of the parking space. Then she entered the dining hall, both nervous and excited about the study.

Catalina greeted her as if she were family. She supposed she was, in a way. Each woman hugged her before River opened with a lovely prayer. Then they read a passage from Matthew 19.

"Peter asked Jesus who could be saved," River said. "Then Jesus replied, 'With men this is impossible, but with God all things are possible.' I know many times I want to latch onto that verse for comfort in hard times. But that's not really the context."

Brisa read the section before it again.

"Oh!" Jody exclaimed. "This is right after the rich young man chose not to sell everything and follow Jesus."

River smiled.

"Si," Catalina said. "Nothing is more impossible than trying to follow Jesus on our own, no?"

"But with God, we can follow Jesus," River said.

Brisa allowed the words to wrap around her broken heart. Escaping Tristin was the hardest thing she had ever done—and God had provided freedom for her through the accident.

Yet that difficulty seemed like nothing compared to the years she half-heartedly tried to follow Jesus in her own power.

Later that day, in the quiet of her room at her parents' home, she asked God to help her follow Jesus in all things. As she looked for a house. As she started dating again. It seemed like both a big and small step at the same time.

4

FRIDAY AFTERNOON, DYLAN sat in his office logging bills of sale and updating feeding schedules when he heard voices in the alleyway. He set aside the papers and walked toward the sound.

"Brisa is home," Harley Franco said.

Dylan stopped short, still hidden in his office, heart thudding against his rib cage.

"Her son Braden is with her."

Papi's laughter floated toward him. "You became a grandfather before either of us. Congratulations!"

"Where is his father?" Uncle Diego asked.

"Gone."

"As in skipped out?"

Harley's voice lowered, and Dylan couldn't hear the answer. His stomach churned as he edged closer to the doorway. He really shouldn't eavesdrop, but he wanted to know more about Brisa.

"Thanks for giving her a job."

Papi grunted. "Renata wouldn't have hired her if she wasn't qualified and you know it."

"Yeah, I know. Still, it's good to know she has a steady income."

Uncle Diego's horse nickered. Dylan recognized the sound. He knew the nuances of each horse, even those that didn't live here, but visited often, like Gold.

"Braden is happy. Surprisingly positive given his... Amputated legs." Harley coughed.

The air rushed from Dylan's lungs as his heart squeezed tight. He staggered as he leaned back against the wall. That must have been Brisa he saw last week with the wheelchair. Poor Brisa, losing her husband. Left to carry such a burden on her own.

"She is looking for a house in Forepaugh. One that we can make wheelchair accessible."

A niggling of guilt rose in his chest. He really should stop listening to the private conversation.

"Let us know how we can help. I can still swing a sledgehammer," Papi said.

"And I hang drywall faster than him," Uncle Diego bragged.

"I'm sure the boys will help, too. Dylan for sure."

Papi knew his character well. Hopefully, he didn't suspect Dylan's secret crush.

"Heidi is out with her and Braden looking at houses today."

The sound of the metal latch locking into place echoed down the aisle as Harley continued.

"It breaks my heart watching her. She loves that little boy. Yet simple things, like getting out of the house in the morning, are so much harder."

Dylan's conscience pricked, knowing she had arrived early the last few days to teach him meditation. He had unknowingly added to her troubles.

Harley snorted. "She makes it look easy, though. She did this on her own for six months before coming home."

"Harley, you've got to let her be independent, if that's what she wants." Papi's voice sounded further away.

The three friends must be grooming their horses and going out for a ride.

Dylan rested his head against the wall for a moment. Brisa had gone through a lot, from the sounds of it. And she was back looking to put down roots.

He swallowed as dryness coated his tongue. The woman he had secretly loved from a distance planned to stay. Maybe...

"Dyl, you in here?" Adan's voice gave just enough warning for Dylan to hurry back to his desk.

"Yup."

"You seen the feed chart?"

Dylan handed him the paper. Adan took it and paused, eyebrows raised and a half-smile on his face.

"Have you ever thought about online dating?" Adan asked.

Dylan's stomach tightened at his friend's question. "No. Have you forgotten my stutter? No one would want me."

Adan frowned. "Not all women are so vain. Besides, you've got the good-looking, mysterious cowboy vibe going for you."

Dylan snorted. "I don't think my face will make up for my speech."

"Let me see your phone."

"Why?" he asked with narrowed eyes. Sounded like another one of Adan's crazy ideas.

"I signed you up for a dating app. Wrote a profile for you. Bragged about all your fine qualities. I just need to install the app for you."

Dylan's throat constricted. His neck and shoulders tightened as he remembered the taunting chants from school.

"Hand it over."

Dylan reluctantly gave his phone to his friend, knowing Adan would probably send his profile to women online without his permission if he didn't. At least this way, he could maintain some control over the situation. He knew Adan intended it to be a good thing.

"You can swipe through the list of eligible single women in our area. It's got filter criteria too. Like if you want a cowgirl, you search for only cowgirls."

"This is a bad idea." There had only been one girl he had wanted to date.

"You're not getting younger. Don't you want to find a wife?"

Thirty-one didn't feel too old to him. Besides, dating involved talking to women — something he failed at miserably. Horses? No problemo. His brothers and his best friend? Same thing. But with women, his tongue knotted up. Strange sounds came from his throat and his words made little sense. Though maybe the morning meditation would help.

"Come on. Here's one. Cowgirl. Thirty. She looks good too. Has all her teeth and everything."

Adan handed his phone back to him.

"She's pretty."

Nothing like Brisa. Not something Dylan could voice aloud without fear of getting decked by Adan.

Yeah. That was just how Dylan's life went. He had had a huge crush on Brisa since high school. He and Adan were two years ahead of her. When she was a sophomore… Wow. She was beautiful.

He had wanted to ask her to the prom, but Adan wasn't shy about his protectiveness. Told him once if a senior dated his sophomore sister, he would lay the guy out.

Though Adan did not know about Dylan's feelings, Dylan didn't chance it. He pined over his friend's younger sister for years. More than a decade. He was hopeless.

Dylan stuffed his phone into his shirt pocket before sitting behind his desk.

"I'm serious Dylan. I'm going out with a girl from the app tonight."

"Your ugly mug?"

"You know women find me irresistible."

Dylan snorted. His female cousins mentioned how fine-looking they thought Adan was. More than once.

"Good luck," he said.

"You should try it. What do you have to lose?"

His dignity. Brisa.

Who was he kidding? Brisa had enough on her plate and had no inkling of Dylan's feelings. He would never have the courage to ask her out, anyway.

After Adan left, Dylan walked to his truck. As he placed his phone in the holder, it flashed on before fading to black after a few seconds.

He picked up his phone and stared at the app. Then he tapped on his profile. He carefully read it to make sure Adan hadn't embellished it. Not bad. Scary how well his friend knew him. The picture of him was from today. Must have snapped it when his head tilted down as he groomed a palomino. The shadow of his cowboy hat obscured most of his face, except for his clean-shaven chin.

Dylan's shoulders rose and fell with his breath. Would it hurt to see who was out there? Maybe God would grant him the ability to speak for one date—just long enough for some mystery woman to fall in love with him. Or at the very least, decide she liked him enough for a second date.

He swiped through the profiles for ten minutes when a photo caught his attention. He would recognize those blue eyes anywhere. His heart pounded hard against his chest— harder than it did breaking a green horse. He could practically hear it. He held his breath as he scanned her profile.

Single cowgirl returning home. Looking for a handsome, chivalrous cowboy to sweep me off my feet. The right man will love his mama, treat women well, and not mind going to cowboy church. If you like an outgoing gal with strong family values and will wait for marriage, message me.

Dylan's throat went dry. Without thinking through his next action, he responded with his profile.

The second it was too late to back out, his stomach clenched. Bile rose in his throat. What had he done? No way she would respond.

He coughed. What if she did?

He groaned as he dropped his phone into his shirt pocket. Then he downed the rest of his bottle of water before he turned on his truck. The engine hummed as he backed out of his spot. He drove over to the bunkhouse for a quick shower before heading to the dining hall. Right as he entered the building, his phone pinged.

Brisa had responded! *Wish I could see your face. Do you have a big scar or something? That doesn't matter to me. I like your profile, though. Sounds like you are close to your family.*

Dylan's throat worked as his heart raced. She liked his profile. Could he really have a chance with her?

His thumbs hovered over the keyboard. *No scars on my face. My mother says I'm a handsome guy. She might be biased.*

When the typing indicator flashed, he held his breath, waiting for her response.

HOUSE HUNTING WITH a four-year-old could try anyone's patience. So Brisa cut herself some slack. She probably could have found someone to babysit Braden, though she worried about how a sitter might handle his disability. It was one thing to ask family for help. Quite another if the sitter was a stranger.

"I liked that house," Mom said as she struggled to collapse the wheelchair so it would fit in the trunk.

Once Braden sat in his booster seat, Brisa snapped the belt over his hips. Mom finally figured out the chair and stowed it. Brisa released a soft breath. Good. Mom would feel better about going out with Braden if she learned how to take care of him.

Brisa slid behind the wheel of her Rav4. Then she backed out and pointed her car toward the highway.

"Yeah, the kitchen is beautiful. Recently remodeled. And the lower peninsula bar is the perfect height for his chair."

"What about the price?" Mom asked. "Is what *that man* left you enough?" The acid in her tone grated against Brisa's already thin nerves.

"Careful, Mom. *That man* is someone's father."

Mom's entire body lifted and sagged in the passenger seat as she expelled a loud sigh. "I'm sorry, Bri. After what you told me, I have a hard time thinking good thoughts about him."

"Yeah, well, he can't hurt me anymore." Or Braden.

"It's enough for a sizable down payment. It'll keep the mortgage low enough that I can afford it."

She hoped. Renata informed her they could not guarantee full-time hours during the summer months. That was eight months away. Hopefully she could save up extra by then. Or pick up some private clients.

"Dad said he knew where to find cheap labor and materials." Their last name probably began with a "V" and they lived on a nearby ranch.

"I'm certain Adan and Dylan will help. Maybe some of Dylan's brother's too."

"It's peak season for them. I won't expect it."

"You know them. They'll call a volunteer day and ten burly men will show up to help you."

Brisa smiled. "Along with Catalina and enough food to feed thirty."

Mom laughed. "Exactly."

When she pulled into their driveway, her phone buzzed. She glanced at the notification from the dating app. She hadn't expected a response at all. Certainly not the same day she posted her profile.

What had she been thinking again?

That's right. It had been Mom's idea. Six months was more than long enough to get over Tristin. As Mom had said, she should allow herself a chance for new love.

Brisa unbuckled Braden from his booster and propped him on her hip. Mom wheeled the chair over and Brisa set him on it. Since Mom held the handles, Brisa let her push him into the house while she locked her car.

New love or first love? Sometimes she wondered if there had been a time she loved Tristin. She didn't fool herself into believing he had ever loved her. No, his actions made that abundantly clear.

Brisa forced the depressing thoughts into a back corner of her mind, where she buried all memories of him.

Once inside the house, she helped Braden sit on a mat in the living room. She handed him a bucket of legos before she hurried upstairs to the privacy of her childhood room.

At last, she tapped on the dating app notification. Another step forward. New house. New job. Maybe a new man.

Brisa's heart fluttered as she studied the man's profile. He loved his family. Was close to his parents and brothers. Worked with horses on a big ranch near Wickenburg. And he loved her profile and her pretty smile.

A twinge of guilt niggled. She hadn't included that she was a single mom in her bio. She hoped that wouldn't come back to haunt her later on. Going forward, she needed to get to know the man before she introduced Braden. Braden had enough to deal with after what they went through with his father. She would make sure any man in her life would be worthy of her and her son long before letting that man know about Braden.

She typed back a message: *Wish I could see your face. Do you have a big scar or something? That doesn't matter to me. I like your profile, though. Sounds like you are close to your family.*

With that taken care of, she called her real estate agent and let her know she wanted to submit an offer for the last house. The perfect little three-bedroom house sat on a nice lot. One big enough for a dog. She had recently read about service dogs that helped amputees. They assisted with mobility and pulled the wheelchair if needed. They could turn lights off and on, retrieve things, and even help dress him. A dog would allow her son more freedom. She planned to get

Braden a service dog as soon as she could afford it.

Besides the lot size, the openness of the rooms would allow effortless movement in a wheelchair. Some doorways needed widened. But there were no long or narrow hallways. The single-story house included an owner's suite, complete with a walk-in shower with no door. She could replace the curb at the shower entrance with a small ramp. The guest bath could remain relatively untouched. The low tub would be fine for bath time. As Braden grew up, she could install grab bars if he wanted to use the shower in there. If not, he could use the shower in her room. She had no immediate plans for the third room. Maybe she could set up her massage table. Then she would have a place for private clients.

The front yard had enough space she could build a ramp and remodel the front porch. Same for the back patio.

She thanked God for providing the funds to buy the house—life insurance money from Tristin. Tristin had never told her he had listed her as the beneficiary of the policy he had purchased through his employer. He had listed her as an emergency contact, so when he didn't show up to work, they called her. She notified them of his death. Then a few weeks later, the Human Resources associate called her to let her know about the policy. One hundred fifty thousand dollars. It took some time before the money became available. But when it did, she moved out of their apartment, packed up the things she wanted to keep, and moved back to her parents' home.

She couldn't think of a better way to spend the money besides putting it toward a house for her son. She planned to use one hundred twenty thousand for the purchase price of the house, saving ten thousand for renovations. The other twenty went to pay off the final expenses she had put on her credit card. The remaining purchase price of the house would leave her with a small mortgage payment she could easily afford.

A message from the dating app pinged again. She smiled at Wrangler92's response to her comment about having a scar. No scars. Handsome.

She typed back: *I'm sure all mothers are biased. Even without seeing your eyes, I can tell you're handsome.*

WRANGLER92: *How was your day?*

Brisa smiled as she told him about the house. *Putting in an offer. It's perfect for…*

She started to type "us" and switched it to "me". She wasn't ready to admit she was a single mom.

Not too big, but nice yard.

He replied: *Send pictures?*

Warmth wrapped around her heart at his interest in such a mundane thing. *Sure, if they accept my offer, I'll send pics.*

Wrangler said he had a few things to wrap up before turning in for the night. He told her he wanted to talk to her more if she was open to it. When she said she was, he wished her sweet dreams.

As she readied for bed, Brisa couldn't help thinking about how her life finally seemed to turn around. God was good.

5

_____

DYLAN WHISTLED AS he hooked the horse trailer up to his extended cab pickup truck. He still couldn't believe Brisa had responded to his messages on the dating app. She thought he was handsome. His chest tightened a little as he wondered if she would be happy or angry to learn that she knew Wrangler92. That he was her brother's best friend.

Tension corded his shoulder muscles. Adan would be angry. He knew it. Ever since high school, he had been very protective of his sister. Dylan recalled Adan saying how he would deck any senior who tried to date her.

Now Dylan was hoping to do just that. He didn't want to betray Adan, but he also wanted to see where things might go with Brisa. His feelings had grown since seeing her again. The meditation sessions every weekday intensified his feelings even more. He didn't want to give up without seeing where things might go.

Once he finished connecting the wires for the lights to the trailer, he glanced at his phone. No messages this morning.

"You keep looking at that thing," Adan said. "You meet someone?"

Adan's grin would vanish if he knew Dylan waited for his sister's messages.

"I'm talking to a woman."

Adan let out a hoot and slapped him on the back. "Good

for you."

"I'm gonna head out," he said.

"You want me to come with you?" Adan asked.

"Naw. No point in both of us losing a day."

"Text when you're headed back. The mountain road outside of Prescott makes me nervous."

Dylan rolled his eyes. "Okay, *Mom*."

Adan chuckled at his teasing while Dylan slid behind the wheel and drove away.

He punched the satellite radio button and tuned to his favorite Christian music station. The drive to Prescott took about an hour and a half. He stopped to stretch his legs before heading further north to a ranch outside of Chino Valley. When he arrived at the ranch, he parked the truck and trailer. The rancher greeted him as he led a stallion to the corral.

The stallion's shiny, dark brown coat glinted in the sun as he walked around the corral, tail swishing away flies. Dylan studied the magnificent horse. The rancher told Dylan more about the stallion named Thunder before Dylan entered the corral. While the rancher held the reins, Dylan ran a hand along the horse's withers and down his legs. He checked each hoof. Not seeing anything of concern, he purchased Thunder before loading him into the trailer.

Once on the road again, he unwrapped the sandwich the chef made for him that morning and nibbled on it, finishing it before the long, winding descent from the mountain to the valley. With the added weight of the horse in the trailer, he carefully feathered the brakes while driving down the steep decline. Though the road was two lanes, some spots narrowed a little too much for his comfort. He had driven this stretch many times and always breathed easier when the road flattened in the valley.

No matter how many times he saw it, the breathtaking view from the valley floor always left him in awe. Looking into the distance, he could see the mountains surrounding the valley, their outlines drenched in shades of light blue. As the sun blazed overhead, the grasses on the valley floor gleamed like burnished gold.

Dylan glanced in the rearview mirror. Thunder looked calm in the trailer. Good. Sometimes an unfamiliar trailer stressed some horses.

Though he could use another trail horse for the resort, he purchased Thunder as a cattle horse. The rancher said the horse did well with cattle and stayed calm even when they ran ATVs near the horses. All good signs that Thunder would be a reliable horse for any of the seasonal cowboys.

Regardless, Dylan would work with Thunder for a few weeks, just to be certain. He preferred giving the horse time to acclimate to his new home before pressing him into service.

By the time he arrived back at the ranch, the sun hung low in the sky, splaying it with orange and red hues. Adan greeted him and unloaded Thunder, volunteering to groom and feed him. Dylan parked the trailer and unhitched it before driving toward the dining hall. As he shut off his truck, he noticed Brisa driving away. Just seeing her small SUV jolted his heart.

He walked into the dining hall, and his stomach grumbled at the sight of the delicious food spread out on the buffet before him. When he saw three of his brothers, Derin, Devon, and Drake, sitting at a table, he joined them.

"Brisa's son is such a cheerful boy," Devon said. "He's so friendly with the guests' kids."

"How do they react to his disability?" Drake asked.

"Better than I expected. Most of them are curious at first. When they play with toys together, the other kids warm up quickly."

"It's got to be a relief for her that he is so well adjusted," Drake said.

Derin shared news from the ranch side of the business. Dylan wondered when he planned to move into his new role as manager over the sports complex. Probably not until the construction finished. In January, he thought.

"Aren't you gonna miss being foreman?" Drake asked.

Derin shrugged. "You know how much I love sports. It will be fun to try something new."

Though his other brothers missed it, Dylan didn't. He heard the hesitation in Derin's voice. Hard to believe his overconfident younger brother might be nervous about his new job. Dylan believed in him. So did Dalton. Derin had always been a charismatic and natural leader. He would be just fine.

Once he finished his meal, Dylan excused himself and headed back to the bunkhouse. He sat on the porch in a rocking chair. The *squick squick* of wood against wood echoed in the night while he messaged Brisa through the dating app.

How was your day?

He breathed deeply of the cool night air while the soothing sound of the rocker rubbing against the porch counted out the seconds until her response came back.

I love my new job. Everyone at the resort is so nice.

He stopped rocking as he thought through his answer. If he really knew nothing about her, he would have asked what resort. So, he played dumb to conceal his identity and asked anyway, a prick of guilt tightening his gut.

Vargas Guest Ranch & Resort. My brother is a cowboy and wrangler there. Our families have been friends for decades. It's so beautiful. I forgot how beautiful while I was gone.

Dylan smiled as he responded he had heard of the place. Then he asked what her job was.

BRISA: *I'm a massage therapist.*

WRANGLER92: *Do you like it?*

BRISA: *Yes. I feel it's a gift. Some clients need a moment of peace away from their busy lives. Others need to let go of anxiety and live in the moment. Some need relief from aches and pains, whether temporary or chronic.*

Dylan never considered all the benefits of a massage, but reading her words, he could tell she was passionate about it.

WRANGLER92: *Sounds like you help many people.*

BRISA: *Yeah. Including a friend of a friend with a speech impediment.*

Dylan's heart pounded hard against his rib cage. She was talking about him.

BRISA: *A speech pathologist asked me to teach him meditation and try to help. I wasn't sure what I could really do, but I'm figuring it out and I think it helps.*

WRANGLER92: *How do you know?*

BRISA: *He seems more relaxed. Haven't heard him stutter once since we started treatment.*

Dylan frowned. She saw him as a patient or a project. He wasn't sure which, but it brought up some of those old feelings from high school—being the freak no one wanted to be friends with. Well, no one besides Adan. A juvenile part of him wanted to ask if Wrangler92 should be worried about this guy. He let it go.

WRANGLER92: *You said you were gone. How long? Where were you?*

Three little dots indicated she was typing a response. He waited for what seemed like forever for it to show up.

BRISA: *I lived in North Phoenix for the last ten years. My ex boyfriend and I had a place together. I worked in Scottsdale.*

His heart pounded when the three dots appeared again.

BRISA: *It might shock you to learn I lived with him. I was far from God. Not making smart decisions. About a year ago, I started going to church again. Looked for a clean break.*

Dylan already knew she had a son with him, so her revelation didn't shock him as much as it would have under other circumstances. Clearly, he had wrongly assumed she had been married to Braden's dad.

WRANGLER92: *Glad you found your way back.*

BRISA: *Thanks. God made a way when I thought there was no way.*

Dylan's brow wrinkled. He wondered what she meant, but didn't want to come across as invasive. Instead, he shared a little about himself. That he had been working in the stables at the same ranch since high school. She asked a few questions before signing off.

Talking to Brisa like this was so freeing. Much easier than stumbling and choking on his words. Maybe after they learned more about each other, she would like him. Then he would meet her in person.

Until then, he really enjoyed getting to know her better without all the stress of his speech impediment. Or her treating him like a project because of it.

Brisa texted Wrangler92 every evening after putting Braden to bed. It seemed to work with Wrangler's schedule, too. She teased him about the number ninety-two on his handle—telling him she hoped it wasn't his age. He confirmed it was his birth year. He was thirty-one. The same age as Adan. And Dylan.

Two years older wasn't bad at all. She wondered if he had ever been married or if he had children. She inwardly cringed as she massaged her client's back. Brisa needed to tread lightly with questions that could turn around on her. She wasn't ready to tell Wrangler about her son. With all they had gone through with Tristin, she wanted to be certain Wrangler's character matched his profile before discussing her son with him.

After the session ended and she swapped out the sheets on her massage table, Brisa headed toward the dining hall for a late lunch. As she picked up a bagged lunch, she noticed River sitting at a table typing away on her laptop. When River looked up and smiled, Brisa asked to join her.

"So," River started. "You're helping Dylan in the morning?"

She sighed as she eased into a chair. Her sore feet thanked her for the break after a busy morning.

"Yeah, I wasn't sure about it at first."

"Why not? He's a great guy."

Brisa swallowed a bite of food, willing her brow not to furrow. "He always seemed standoffish when I knew him in high school."

River's head jerked back slightly. "Really? I mean, he's quiet. Shy. But it seems like he really cares about the people in his life."

Brisa considered her words. "Maybe. I know he loves horses. And he is nice enough when he drives us to and from a scenic spot for meditation."

River closed her laptop and slid it slightly away from her before sipping an iced coffee drink. "But?"

"He says hardly anything."

River nodded sympathetically. "He's spent his life enduring judgment and derision for his stuttering. Can you really blame him?"

The question stabbed at Brisa's conscience. River was right. How many times had she worried Braden would face similar ridicule when he started school?

"I guess not."

When Brisa asked about River, it surprised her to learn River was a semi-famous romance author.

"I write cowboy romances now," River said.

"Was Dalton your inspiration?"

River's cheeks turned pink. "Yeah, kinda."

"You seem happy together."

"We are."

Brisa stuffed down her envy. Though she had never been interested in any of the Vargas men, she knew they were upstanding, honest men full of integrity. Well, except maybe Derin. He had a reputation of being a player. She wished she had chosen a man like the other Vargas brothers instead of enduring Tristin's manipulative games and rough treatment.

"What is it?" River asked.

"Sorry. Just thinking about Braden's dad."

"And they aren't happy memories?"

Brisa snorted. "Our life is significantly better without him. Not that I wished him dead." She didn't. But that was the means God provided for her escape.

For a moment, she debated telling River the whole ugly truth about her old life with Tristin. Instead, she glanced at her watch. She had plenty of time, but not enough courage.

"My next client will arrive soon, so I should go. It was nice talking with you."

River smiled, her entire face lighting up. "My pleasure. And if you ever want to talk about it, I would love to listen."

Brisa stood and crumpled her sandwich bag in her hand. Surely she could trust River. Nothing she had shared at Bible study left the group. Maybe it would be good to confide in a friend. Though now wasn't the time.

"Thanks. I'll keep that in mind."

After dropping her wrapper in the trash, she waved to River. Then she walked along the gravel walkway between the dining hall and the resort, toward the spa. The sun warmed her back and a light breeze tickled her neck. The trees along the path provided intermittent shade. Bright mounds of lantana added joyful pops of yellow, lavender, and orange between stretches of desert dirt and landscaping gravel. A hibiscus hedge with bright pink flowers provided privacy for the first-floor rooms with a patio facing the courtyard.

Brisa kicked a rock off the pathway, stuffing her hands in her pockets. The old familiar guilt gnawed at her heart. Had she left Tristin this time last year, Braden would still have his legs. It was her fault her son would live his life with a disability.

She had almost made it that time. Had a suitcase packed

with clothes and necessities for her and Braden. Tristin hadn't been due home for another hour. It should have been enough time for her to load her son and their most important belongings into her Rav.

A tear trickled down her cheek. She sniffed and brushed the back of her hand over her eyes. Tristin had arrived home early, catching Brisa as she loaded the suitcase into her trunk. She had already buckled Braden into his booster seat.

Tristin had been furious. He pulled his sports car into the lot, his brakes smoking with his abrupt stop right behind her. He had left his car door open as he strode toward her. His violent shove knocked her into the side of her hatchback trunk opening. A bruise formed almost instantly on her face. His fingers dug into the skin of her upper arm as he yanked her away from her car. Dragging her behind him, he rushed to the apartment door, unlocked it and pushed her so hard she fell against the cold tile.

More tears streamed down her face as the memory came back. Brisa found a bench and sat, burying her face in her hands.

Ten minutes. All she had needed was ten more minutes, and she would have been free from his violent temper and harsh treatment. Ten minutes would have put her on the freeway, headed home to a family that loved her.

Instead, she suffered through that dreadful night and many more for five more months. Until God rescued her and Braden through Tristin's death.

The flood of emotions washed over Brisa in waves. Guilt. Fear. Regret. Remorse.

Lord!

Her prayer faltered, choked out by her shame. She didn't deserve a new life. She didn't deserve forgiveness. Braden's loss reminded her of that daily.

With her face still covered, she sensed someone's presence next to her. A large, masculine hand rubbed circles on her back between her shoulder blades. The man said nothing, only offered silent comfort.

When she finally regained control of herself, Brisa looked up. Shock socked her hard in the chest—for none other than Dylan Vargas sat next to her.

She blinked and launched to her feet, hurrying down the path back to the spa. How embarrassing that he had come across her in the throes of a breakdown. Couldn't it have been someone she didn't know?

Suddenly, she felt humbled. A man who she had completely misjudged offered her comfort amid her heartbreak. She should have thanked him instead of fleeing. Next time she saw him, she would.

6

ON FRIDAY EVENING, Dylan left for the day with just enough time to shower before driving over to the dining hall for supper. As he pushed the door open, the chatter of people and the clinking of silverware greeted him, filling the room with a lively hum. The smell of fresh herbs and spices wafted from the chafing dishes, mingling with the smoky aroma of roasted meat. His stomach growled as he joined the long buffet line.

With a plate piled full of mouthwatering food, Dylan searched the room for an open seat. It surprised him to find Brisa and Braden sitting with Adan. He smiled as he ambled toward them. Adan noticed him and waved him over.

"You should join us," Adan said.

"I'd love to."

"You know Brisa," Adan said. "This is my nephew, her son. Braden, this is Dylan. He's my bestest friend in the entire world."

After setting his plate on the table in front of the empty chair, Dylan crouched at Braden's eye level. "Nice to meet you."

When Braden said nothing, Brisa prompted him as she rested a hand on the top of his downy hair. "What do you say?"

"Hi." Braden lowered his head. "No legs."

Dylan's eyes snapped to Brisa's face at her sharp intake

of air. Her eyes rounded in horror and he quickly thought through how to fix the situation.

"That's okay. I sometimes st-st-stutter," he said, placing a hand on her son's arm. "B-b-but Jesus loves us, anyway."

Braden cautiously looked up at him, eyes earnest. "He does?"

"Yes. He does."

A grin broke across Braden's face. Brisa's eyes reddened, and she dug in her purse, pulling out a tissue. As she blotted her face dry, Dylan's heart squeezed. The desire to hold her shot through him, just like it had earlier in the week when he came upon her crying on a bench. He longed to take her pain away.

When Adan cleared his throat, Dylan quickly dropped his hand to his side, and his eyes shifted to his friend in time to catch his slightly narrowed eyes. Did he suspect Dylan had feelings for Brisa? Dylan hoped not.

"We thought we'd stay for the hayride tonight," Brisa said, her shaky voice growing more confident with each word.

Dylan plopped down on the empty chair. He bowed his head for a few seconds to pray over his meal. While he ate, he listened to their conversation about Brisa's house.

"When is your closing date?" Adan asked.

"Two more weeks. I've been bookmarking pictures of accessible ramps for the front and back. I still have so much to figure out."

"How can I help?" Dylan asked.

Brisa shrugged. "I'm not sure how much I can do before I get the keys."

"Do you have a general contractor?" Adan asked.

"Dad gave me the number for a buddy of his who I can ask questions. Unfortunately, I can't..." She glanced at Braden. "A general contractor isn't in my budget."

Dylan tucked that bit of information away for later. Somehow, he would help.

As he finished his meal, Brisa asked Adan when the hayride would start. They still had about a half hour before the first one. Thankfully, he and Adan no longer had to man the hayrides, like past years. This year, he had hired local college-age workers for the job, with Parker Quaid supervising.

"Do you want to walk around while we wait?" Adan asked.

She agreed, so he stood and held her chair for her. Adan wheeled Braden next to Brisa. Dylan fell into step beside her, itching to twine his fingers with hers. He jammed his hand in his pocket to keep himself from such foolishness.

The deep navy blue of twilight swathed a canopy over them as the solar lights cast a golden glow along the sidewalk between the resort buildings. His long sleeves were perfect for the cool evening. No jackets needed yet. In a few weeks, they might need a lightweight one. He enjoyed when the weather turned cooler.

Brisa told them about her house, most of which Dylan already knew—well, Wrangler92 knew. Guilt slithered around his conscience. The longer he delayed meeting her in person, the more likely he was to slip up.

But texting Brisa came easy. No stutters or facial tics ruining his image. He shared his heart and soul with her and received no judgment in return.

Adan cleared his throat. "We should probably head over now."

Dylan led them to the line for the hayrides. They only waited a few minutes before a wagon became available. Adan parked Braden's chair next to a stack of pumpkins and a scarecrow. Solana had outdone herself with all the harvest themed decorations.

The sweet scent of hay filled Dylan's nostrils as he climbed into the wagon. He held his hand out for Brisa. She took it as she stepped up. Tingles shot up his arm, sending his pulse racing. As soon as she released his hand, he missed the feel of her soft, lithe fingers against his rough ones. He offered her a spot and sat next to her. Adan carried Braden over and when Braden reached for Brisa, she held him in her lap. Adan sat on her other side.

"Do you like horses?" Braden asked. "Uncle Adan works with horses."

"Yes," Dylan answered. "I like horses. I work with your uncle in the stables."

Braden's eyes widened. "Do you ride 'em?"

Dylan smiled. "Yes. I even have one of my own."

"You do?"

Adan chuckled. "Technically, he owns all of them."

"Can I have a horse?" Braden craned his neck to see his mother's face.

Dylan noticed Brisa's back stiffen as the wagon pulled away from the loading area.

"I don't think so, cowpoke," Adan said, ruffling his hair.

While Braden peppered Adan with questions, Dylan wondered how much it would cost to buy a special saddle for Braden. He decided he would investigate how to teach him to ride despite his disability. Clearly, the little boy would love it.

BRISA BREATHED DEEPLY, the scent of hay mixed with Dylan's musky cologne. He smelled amazing. And his attentiveness towards her son stirred her heart deeply, especially after he had reassured her son of Jesus's love earlier. She still couldn't believe Braden said that about his legs.

Thankfully, neither he nor Adan promised Braden riding lessons. She couldn't bring herself to squelch Braden's interest in horses, though with his disability, she doubted he could ever ride.

The jingle of the harnesses and the occasional whiffle

from the horses punctuated the night. Brisa swayed, matching the motion of the wagon. The stars sparkled overhead, growing in number as they rode further away from the lights of the resort. Dylan shifted Braden to his lap and pointed out a few constellations.

Braden asked Dylan something, and he leaned closer, whispering in her son's ear. Whatever he said caused Braden to giggle and Dylan to smile. Dylan rubbed a hand on Braden's belly and more laughter floated in the clear night air. Adan glanced up from his phone, half-smile on his face, before he went back to texting his online girlfriend.

Brisa wanted to memorize the sweet way Dylan treated her son. The scene was so foreign to her life a year ago. The thought sent shivers up her back. No, she wouldn't ruin the perfect moment thinking about Tristin. She was done with him and all he represented. He couldn't hurt them any more.

"Cold?" Dylan asked.

When Brisa rubbed her hands over her arms, Dylan settled Braden on his other leg before slinging his arm behind her, resting his palm on the hay bale. Pleasant warm waves moved through her body, banishing any chill. Adan's phone illuminated his face. He still appeared engrossed in his text conversation as the wagon slowed, nearing the drop-off point.

"Who is up for s'mores by the bonfire?" Dylan asked, his dark eyes dancing with delight.

Brisa's heart thrummed. She definitely wanted to stay there with him longer.

"I want s'mores!" Braden shouted as Adan ruffled his hair.

"I gotta run," Adan said as he dropped his phone into his shirt pocket. A grin spread across her brother's face. "Got a hot date."

"Go." She playfully shoed him away.

Adan wheeled Braden's chair over before he left.

"Hang tight," Dylan said to Braden, "while I help your

mom down."

Dylan jumped over the side of the wagon with ease. The action caused Brisa's heart rate to speed. Suddenly, she was no longer chilled. When he offered her his hand, she placed hers in it as she stepped down. Then he climbed back up and handed Braden down to her. She settled him in his chair.

"S'mores, Mommy!"

"Mmm. Sounds good," she said in a cheery tone.

Then Dylan led them over to the bonfire.

Brisa matched his casual stride, very aware of everything about him. She studied Dylan with fresh eyes. He stood over half a foot taller than her, something she had never noticed before. Just like she hadn't noticed his strong, angular jaw or his soft eyes full of joy. The definition of the muscles in his broad shoulders were visible through the fitted forest green henley. Even his end-of-the-day stubble added to his masculine appeal.

As they neared the firepit, they accepted the gram crackers, chocolate, marshmallows, and roasting sticks from a teenage girl. Brisa remembered seeing her during the seasonal worker orientation the other day. Dylan speared two marshmallows on a stick and helped Braden hold it near the flame.

She rolled her eyes at his slow technique. "I prefer the flame-and-melt method."

Dylan laughed. "We're more refined. We don't like the burnt sugar taste. Isn't that right?"

"Yeah!" Braden exclaimed.

She threaded her marshmallows on the stick and quickly caught them on fire. Then she held them up, blowing puffs of air on them to put out the flame before building her s'more.

"Wanna bite, baby?"

Dylan's gaze locked on hers, smoldering as hot as her charred marshmallow. Though she intended the question for her son, Brisa broke off a piece for him. When Dylan opened his mouth, she dropped it in. His lips brushed softly against her fingertips, sending electricity zinging between them. Her breath caught. What was wrong with her? This was Dylan Vargas. Adan's best friend. She tried to deny any attraction towards him.

"Oh, no!" Braden's lament broke the moment. "It falled in the fire."

"Sorry, buddy. Let's try again," Dylan said, waving the teenager over for more marshmallows.

Brisa nibbled on her now cold s'more, still a little breathless from Dylan's nearness. She wasn't in her right mind. This was the quiet, aloof Dylan. But also the man who said those wonderful things to Braden. The man who genuinely enjoyed spending time with her son. Teaching him about the constellations. Answering his curious questions.

Dylan was the kind of man she wanted as Braden's father. A man of integrity. Kind and caring for her and her son. The thought gave her pause. She shouldn't think about Adan's best friend that way, should she?

When the second set of marshmallows was lightly golden brown, Dylan proclaimed them ready for the sweet sandwich. He put the parts together and handed a third of it to Braden, eating the rest himself.

As Braden ate a bite, his eyes rounded. "Mmm. Good!" he exclaimed around a mouthful.

"Chew it, baby."

Part of the sticky marshmallow stuck to his cheek. Brisa hid her laughter behind her hand.

Dylan glanced at her, red coloring his face. "Um. You match."

Heat warmed her cheeks as she patted her face, trying to find the smear.

By now, Braden's fingers and face wore several marshmallow dots. Thankfully, the teenager stopped by with some wet wipes. Brisa rubbed the remnants of s'more from her son's skin, her heart light.

When she turned her attention back to Dylan, his arm raised slowly, loosely gripping a wet wipe. Her smile faded, and her breath left in a soft whoosh. The damp towelette lightly brushed across her cheek. She let her eyes travel over Dylan's features as he removed the marshmallow streak.

"Thank you," she whispered.

His Adam's apple bobbed up and down as he visibly swallowed. His arm dropped to his side, but those handsome chocolate eyes held her gaze for a million heartbeats.

"Anytime."

She swayed closer to him, as if caught in a trance.

Braden yanked on her arm, interrupting what could have been. His mouth stretched wide with a yawn. "Mommy, I'm tired."

Brisa held back a sigh. She couldn't remember the last time she enjoyed herself so much and she wasn't ready to go home. Or to leave Dylan's company. But it was past Braden's bedtime.

"I should take him home."

Dylan smiled and squeezed her hand, sending bolts of lightning up her arm.

"Let me walk you to your car."

Dylan wheeled Braden toward the car for her. After she set him in his booster seat, she buckled the hip strap while Dylan folded up the wheelchair. Once he stowed it in the trunk, he walked with her to the driver's door, holding it open for her. She eased into the seat, still holding his gaze. He propped his arm on the edge of the door.

"Good night, Brisa." His deep voice wrapped around her heart as he closed the door. She watched him walk away before she drove home, still wondering what had just happened between her and Dylan Vargas. Whatever it was, she liked it.

7

IT TOOK EVERY ounce of Dylan's self-control not to kiss Brisa after he walked her to her car. She looked amazing, with her blond hair framing her face in delicate waves. For a moment, he thought she felt the intense connection, too. Dare he hope?

As he parked at the bunkhouse, he considered messaging her through the dating app. But he didn't know what to. He wasn't ready to reveal his true identity.

At last, Dylan opened the app and typed: *Been thinking about you all day. Sorry so busy this evening. Sweet dreams.*

Then he closed the app, not waiting for a reply. She was probably still driving home, anyway. Then he eased out of his truck, entered the bunkhouse, and changed into sleep shorts and a loose t-shirt.

As he stretched out on his bed, Devon sat on the corner near his feet, concern etched on his brow. Even though Dylan was seven years older, he had always been close to Devon. Perhaps it was because of his gentle nature and keen mind. He could often find Dev with his nose in a book. Out of all the Vargas brothers, he was the smartest. Dylan always thought Dev would leave the ranch and find another career. He could see his brother as a high school history teacher.

"So... Brisa Franco, huh?"

Dylan's eyes darted around the room to make sure they were alone. Derin's loud groan came from the living room.

Sounded like they were watching a pro bull riding competition. Strange that Derin had stayed home on a Friday night with the resort at full occupancy. Surely, Derin could find some pretty woman to charm. Dylan couldn't think of a single Friday night since Derin moved to the bunkhouse nine years ago where Derin had stayed in. Odd.

"We're alone." Devon's voice drew him back to his question. "I saw you on the hayride with your arm around her. And with Adan sitting right there. Bold move."

Bold? More like foolish. At the last second, he had placed his hand on the hay bale instead of her waist, like he wanted. Heat burned his face as his jaw twitched.

"Adan was texting his internet girlfriend the whole time. He didn't notice." He hoped.

"Are you dating Brisa?"

Dylan's eyes snapped to his brother's. Then he rubbed a hand over his face. "It's c-c-complicated."

Devon's eyes rounded, and his back straightened.

"I'm dating her online. Wrangler92, the profile Adan created for me." Dylan cleared his throat. "She doesn't know it's me. Adan knows I'm talking to a woman. He just doesn't know it's her."

"Dylan! This won't end well. You must tell her."

Dylan looked away. "You wouldn't understand."

"It's the stutter, isn't it?"

Dylan nodded. "Texting her, I can be myself. Speak intelligently. Joke around. Flirt with her. Wish her sw-sw-sweet dreams without feeling like an idiot."

"You know you have to come clean. It's not fair to let her believe she doesn't know you. Especially if she might have feelings for you—you in the flesh or you online."

Dylan huffed. "She doesn't have feelings for the real me."

Devon raised an eyebrow. "Are you sure? I saw something between you when you were making s'mores."

Dylan deflected. "Aren't you too young to know about

women?"

Devon scoffed. "I'm twenty-four. I've dated a little."

It was Dylan's turn to be surprised.

"Hey. We're not talking about me. We're talking about you. Be careful. I can tell you like her a lot. Remember, there are more than just your feelings at stake. There's hers, Adan's, and a heartbroken little boy's. A little boy desperate for a dad's love."

Dylan's chest tightened, and his throat constricted. Devon was right. The stakes were much higher than he had considered.

"I'm gonna watch the rodeo for a while before I turn in," Devon said. "I hope everything works out for you."

Now what? It was too soon to meet Brisa in person. She still hadn't mentioned Braden to Wrangler92. Did that mean she didn't trust him yet?

If he didn't play this right, he could lose her forever. That thought sent a rush of fear through his body. He couldn't lose her.

No, he would keep getting to know her in the app until she opened up more. Then he would find the right time. Meet her for dinner. Tell her everything. But not until he knew for certain she liked him.

BRISA SLEPT IN on Saturday morning, a rare occurrence. She glanced at her nightstand for the old-school baby monitor she had found at a yard sale for a steal. She had never expected to need it at Braden's age. Until he became strong enough to either walk on his stumps or push himself in a wheelchair to the bathroom at night, the monitor seemed the best solution. It was gone. She darted upright. Had she forgotten to bring it into her room?

Braden's giggles floated up the stairs through her

cracked door. Brisa eased back against her pillows. Her mom or dad must have gotten up with him. He was fine.

Her phone flashed on and she noticed the notification from the dating app. As she reached for her phone, she paused, remembering the way Dylan made her feel last night. So many sweet moments passed between them. She tucked her arm under her pillow and stared at her phone.

Dylan Vargas. Who would have ever believed he would be the man to set her pulse on fire and trap butterflies in her stomach? One of the Vargas brothers. A man with a reputation of fairness and compassion.

And Adan's best friend.

Brisa sighed. Pushing the memories away, she unlocked her phone and tapped on the dating app. She read the message Wrangler sent last night. He had been thinking about her all day long. Ugh. He hadn't crossed her mind—not when she had been with Dylan.

His status turned to green. Oh, my! He was online right then. What should she do?

Her heart pounded in her ears. She took a deep breath and typed a message to him.

Morning, handsome. Sorry I missed your message last night. I went on a hayride with my...

She still hadn't mentioned her son. Her finger hovered over the "s" for a second. Without pressing it, she typed "brother," instead.

WRANGLER92: *Did you have fun?*

The half-truths piled up. She should be honest with Wrangler. Wasn't that the right thing to do?

BRISA: *I had a pleasant time. Ate some s'mores. I haven't done that in ages. Probably since high school.*

WRANGLER92: *I didn't do much. Long week. Any news on your house?*

BRISA: *It closes soon. I can't hardly wait. I need to plan a few renovations. Maybe, if you're not busy, you could...*

Brisa stopped. Was she about to suggest he could go

with her to pick up supplies? They hadn't met yet. That sounded like a terrible first date.

She sent an embarrassed face emoji. *Sometimes I forget we haven't met yet. I feel like I know so much about you.*

WRANGLER92: *Me too. Just don't want to rush things. I enjoy being friends first.*

Brisa sighed. Friends first. It sounded like a good idea. Very different from how things progressed with Tristin. Maybe if she wanted a different outcome, approaching the relationship slowly was a good idea.

Wrangler92 typed: *If we had already met, I would offer to help with your remodeling. I'm pretty handy with a hammer and drywall. I can paint too. But I want to get to know you more before we meet. I hope you understand.*

A strange thought knifed her heart. *You aren't married, are you?*

WRANGLER92: *No. Never even kissed a woman. Maybe that's a stupid thing to admit. I always planned to reserve kissing for someone I love. Not just someone I'm attracted to.*

Oh, wow. That definitely sounded slower than she had ever taken things.

WRANGLER92: *I respect women too much to play with their emotions or risk igniting something physical if I don't see the woman as a potential lifelong partner. I suppose it sounds old-fashioned. Probably why I've never dated and why I'm pouring out my soul to you through an app.*

A smile stretched across her face. Old-fashioned didn't scare her. It comforted her after her experience with Tristin. Maybe she could trust Wrangler.

BRISA: *I'm glad you want to take things slow. My ex was... Treated me harshly if you can read between the lines. It was by the grace of God I finally broke free. Slow is exactly what I need.*

Her heart raced as she watched the three dots bounce, waiting for his reply.

WRANGLER92: *Are you safe? Could he find you? Hurt you again?*

BRISA: *I'm safe. He passed away. Car accident early this year.*

WRANGLER92: *Good. I mean, I'm glad you're safe and that he can't hurt you anymore. Sorry to cut this short. Gotta go work with some horses. Talk tonight?*

BRISA: *Yeah. Have a good day.*

WRANGLER92: *You too.*

The status bubble faded to gray. Brisa stared at the conversation for a minute. Wrangler was protective and old-fashioned. Not a problem. His concern for her caused flutters in her stomach.

She shook off the thoughts and readied for her day, knowing she had a long list of things to accomplish with her weekend before she took possession of her new home.

8

WHISTLING, DYLAN ENTERED his office and sat in front of his computer. He had been too busy last week to research horse riding gear for amputees. After typing in a few search terms, he skimmed the results and refined it for young children. Dylan finally discovered the specialized saddles were called therapeutic saddles. He came across a tack maker in another state that made custom saddles for amputees and even paraplegic customers of all ages. Fascinated, he continued reading about the saddler. He took notes about the information the saddle maker needed so he could contact him soon to order a saddle for Braden. No need to trouble Brisa with the expense. Or chance that she would decide not to let Braden ride horses.

With that task completed, he caught up on paperwork until it was time to leave with Adan and Brisa for her new house. He and Adan promised to help her with her plans today so they could start remodeling later in the week. She wanted to move in before Thanksgiving, which didn't give them much time.

"Ready?" Adan asked as Dylan stood, grabbing his keys off his desk.

Brisa offered him a smile before the three of them walked through the stables to the parking lot.

"I'll drive," Dylan said.

"Shotgun!" Brisa tossed over her shoulder with a grin.

Adan nudged her arm, then held the passenger door open for her. "Like I'd be caught dead not offering the front seat to a *girl*."

She chuckled at her brother's teasing, bringing a smile to Dylan's face.

When he opened the driver's side door, Brisa's perfume wafted toward him. He loved that scent. It reminded him of the ocean at sunset. Not that he frequented ocean beaches.

"Let me see your phone," she said. "And I'll plug in the address."

Dylan reluctantly unlocked it and handed it over, hoping she didn't notice the dating app or any notifications from it. He wasn't ready to reveal himself as Wrangler92—and definitely not in front of Adan.

While he pulled out of his parking spot by the stables, the navigation app's voice gave him step-by-step instructions. When it announced they had arrived at their destination, he parked the truck in front of the cutest house he had ever seen. The grin on Brisa's face brought one to his own.

"Congratulations, Brisa."

"Thanks. I can hardly wait for the two of you to see it."

The back door thudded shut and Brisa's door opened as Adan held it for her. Dylan would have enjoyed a few seconds alone with her, but they had a lot to accomplish before the surprise volunteer day on Friday. Dylan had arranged for several cowboys, most of his brothers, and his parents to help. He exited his truck and hustled to Brisa's side as she strolled up the walkway.

"We'll need a ramp in the front. And the back too. But I'll talk about that later."

She held a tablet up for both him and Adan as she swiped through several pictures. "I was thinking something like this. I think we can use a shorter ramp since the front door isn't as far off the ground."

"That looks nice," Dylan said.

"Do you want wood like that or concrete?"

"I can't afford concrete. Dad introduced me to one of his construction buddies, Robert. He was very patient answering all my questions. Turns out concrete work can be pretty expensive."

"How much?" Dylan asked.

She told him and the price sounded reasonable. Something he could easily cover with the money in his checking account.

"Building wood will mean treating it against termites, painting it every few years, and probably replacing it in fifteen," Adan said. "Concrete should be a one and done."

"Yeah, well, I've got a budget to work with," Brisa said. "Even with Robert taking me to the wholesale places to buy supplies, I can't afford concrete."

Dylan opened his mouth and Adan shook his head, giving him the talk-later look they had perfected over the years.

"The porch needs raised to be flush with the doorway too."

Brisa unlocked the front door and entered, followed by him and Adan. Light from the windows filled the large open space.

"Kitchen's nice," Adan said, turning in a circle in the room.

Dylan agreed. The cabinets looked new, and the quartz countertop was in pristine condition. They also updated all the fixtures and appliances.

"That was one of the main reasons I picked this place. The lower bar is the perfect height for Braden. It'll work until I can save up for an actual table."

Dylan's heart squeezed tight. He really wanted to fill the gaps she mentioned. Concrete. Furniture. Whatever else she needed. Only she would not accept his charity and he knew it.

Brisa took them on a tour, describing several other changes. The opening for the two smaller bedrooms needed widened. Brisa mentioned her dad's friend again. Robert gave her a quote on it and ensured her that even though the wall was load-bearing, widening the doorways was still possible.

When they stepped onto the deck in the back, Dylan smiled. He loved the one-acre yard. Though mowing it would be a chore — one he would volunteer to help with — it was the perfect place for children to run and play.

"The fence can probably wait," she said as her shoulders dropped.

Dylan scanned the rotting wood slats, leaning at a precarious angle. Gaps in the fence were large enough for a little boy to wriggle through. He didn't think waiting to replace it was a good idea.

"I was going to build a taller one to contain a service dog, but..."

"But what?" Adan asked.

"I don't think I'll ever be able to afford one. The kind trained for his needs has a four-year wait list and they cost over forty grand."

Dylan's eyes widened. So much money. But it was worth it for little Braden's quality of life.

"That's a lot of money," Adan muttered.

Money that Dylan had in his savings account. As a thirty-one-year-old man who lived in a bunkhouse and whose only major expense was insurance for his truck, he had saved and invested most of his earnings since he turned eighteen. His net worth was well over three million dollars last he checked, not including his share of Vargas Ranch. He could meet a lot of Brisa's needs with that money. He would pray about it. And talk to Adan. Hopefully, Adan would never suspect his real motive for wanting to help Brisa.

"I know. When I first learned about the service dogs, I really wanted to get one for Braden. It would help him grow up more independently. Let him be more like a normal boy."

Dylan heard her suppressed sob. He longed to pull her close and comfort her. Instead, he jammed his hands in his pockets, heart aching with her.

"The blades—artificial limbs—would also help. Those are expensive too. So, we're stuck with the wheelchair until I can find some way to pay for all of it. Or find a charity willing to help."

An idea sparked. A charity. One he could start and run on the side. Except for one major problem. His stupid stutter. No one would want to donate to a charity with an incompetent sounding leader.

Somehow, he would find a way to help Brisa anonymously. If it led to helping others in her situation, so be it. If not, he would settle for helping just her and Braden.

Brisa continued rattling off her renovation needs. When she finished, he drove her home. Adan hopped in the front seat for the drive back to the ranch.

"I saw your wheels turning, Dyl. She will not take your charity."

"What if I started a non-profit?"

Adan snorted. "Get out of my head, bro."

Dylan jerked his gaze to Adan's for a second before turning his attention back to the road. "You were thinking it, too?"

"Yeah. I've got a fair amount saved up from my rodeo days. My financial advisor has grown my portfolio, too."

"So, how do we start something?" Dylan asked.

"Don't know. But you know who might?"

He shook his head.

"Your speech pathologist, Shirley."

"Huh?"

"I looked her up online when you told me about her. She started a non-profit for kids with speech impediments that she runs with her granddaughter."

Who knew? "I'll text her when we get back."

"Good, 'cause we're gonna get my sister that dog, those blades, and anything else she needs."

"Horse riding gear."

Adan laughed. "Of course. You've been dying to take him riding, haven't you? Ever since the hayride?"

"He's a little boy who needs the chance to have fun like every other little boy."

"Alright. Let me know what Shirley says. In the meantime, I need to see if Robert can draw up plans the rest of us can follow. Before Friday."

"No pressure," Dylan teased.

ON TUESDAY, DYLAN met with Shirley for his session. The morning meditation helped him a lot, but he knew Shirley would push him outside of his comfort zone again soon.

"Morning!" she greeted him with her usual cheeriness. "I heard there's a trail ride in a half hour. Guess what?"

His stomach clenched. Here it came.

"You're gonna talk to the guests—a group of women business owners."

Dylan swallowed hard as his pulse raced. This could not be happening. Not today. He didn't feel ready.

"They're gorgeous, by the way. Thirty-somethings."

He frowned. "Y-y-you—"

Shirley held up a hand. "Remember what I've taught you."

Dylan closed his eyes and drew in air, filling the bottom of his lungs first. Then he slowly released it through his nose. After the third breath, he opened his eyes.

"You don't play fair, do you?"

Shirley grinned as she patted his hand. "What questions do you usually ask the guests?"

He rattled them off.

"Excellent! Come, then. Let's not keep them waiting."

His shoulders bunched as they walked down the alleyway and out of the stables. Adan stood, chatting up a lovely brunette. He winked at Dylan as he wrapped up his conversation.

Shirley stood next to him, her way of offering moral support, he supposed.

The first question came out with some awkward pauses, but no stuttering. As he listened to their answers, his shoulders loosened. These women didn't know him. They trusted him to know horses.

A blond woman moved from behind the group before the next question. She smiled and his heart danced. Brisa motioned like she did when she reminded him to take deep breaths. He did so and waited a second for his heart rate to slow before asking the next question.

For the third question, his mami peered around the tall women. She smiled and mouthed, "You've got this, mijo."

Shirley Willis was something else. Enlisting people he trusted to help boost his confidence. He owed her more than he could ever repay.

When the women finished answering his questions, he flashed a confident grin and told them to mingle while they readied the horses. He turned toward the stables and faltered. Dalton stood, arms folded over his chest, grinning from ear to ear. His trusty dog leaned against his leg, panting softly. As Dylan walked past him, Dalton squeezed his shoulder.

"I knew you could do it."

"Thanks."

"And we're all here for you until you fully believe it yourself."

Any lingering resentment he held towards his older brother faded away as they worked side-by-side, grooming and saddling the horses. Once the guests were on their way, Dalton followed behind Shirley as she walked to Dylan's office.

"Adan said you want to start a charity," Dalton said.

"I'd like to hear about it too, if you don't mind."

Since the other day, Dylan had thought of little else. Ideas for fundraisers on the ranch. The mission of the charity, and so much more. He shared his ideas with Shirley and Dalton, both eagerly listening to all he said.

"I'd be happy to share some pointers about starting a 501(c)3. Would you run it yourself?" Shirley asked.

"I'm not sure. I don't know how much time it would take."

"My granddaughter has ours running like a fine-tuned machine. She's looking for a new challenge."

"We couldn't steal her away," Dylan said.

"She'll want to take this on, trust me. She's already been mentoring her successor."

Dalton spoke up, "Dylan, I've got to run, but I want you to know River and I would love to contribute. She'll want to volunteer in some capacity, too."

Dylan thanked his brother and took down Shirley's granddaughter's information. He would call Shannon Burke soon. He could hardly wait to put his plan in place.

BRISA SMILED AS Dylan held his truck door open for her. As dawn colored the sky pink and blue, she breathed in the refreshing sixty degree air. She admired her new home, envisioning the changes that would take place that day.

Adan and Drake exited from the back seat of Dylan's truck. Dalton parked behind him. Tres and Catalina emerged from his truck, followed by stacks of food containers. Dalton retrieved a pop-up shade canopy from the bed of his truck and quickly set it up. After Tres set up a folding table under the canopy, Catalina opened a container.

"Breakfast burritos are ready!" she announced in her thick accent.

Adan and Drake veered toward the table. Soon cowboys appeared, burrito in one hand, power tools in the other. Robert and Dad stood by another table, reviewing plans.

Brisa's eyes burned. She had witnessed this group of people in action before. But this time it was *her* home, *her* family in need.

"Some sight, isn't it?" Dylan whispered.

She let out a shaky breath as more trucks arrived. More cowboys moved around the yard like ants, carrying drywall, wood, and other supplies into the house. Several groupings of sawhorses and saws littered the backyard as the sun cast bright rays overhead.

"You did this, didn't you?"

Dylan nodded, staring deep into her eyes. Her heart pounded as she faced him. Stretching up on her tiptoes, she placed a kiss on his cheek. She appreciated his kindness more than she could say.

"You're the best of men, Dylan Vargas. Thank you."

His faced reddened and his eyes darted away as he ducked his head. Then he walked away. Picking up a few tools and supplies, he entered her house.

Brisa noticed his cousin, Solana, so she waved her over.

"Who is watching Braden today?" Solana asked.

"Mom has him at home. She'll take him to his physical therapy appointment this afternoon."

"Rennie apologizes she can't break away."

"No worries. I figured a few folks needed to keep the ranch and resort running."

"Yeah. Derin thinks he can manage the herd himself. Dad called the pastor yesterday and a few friends from church are going to help at the ranch for the day."

Brisa laughed, knowing Derin liked control and had little patience for greenhorns.

When Solana's eyes locked on one cowboy, Brisa realized Solana was staring at Adan. He tossed his checkered shirt over the fence, leaving his white t-shirt stretched taut over his muscles. Brisa snickered to herself. She was used to women drooling over her older brother.

"That should be criminal," Solana muttered under her breath before she turned her attention back to Brisa. "Put me to work."

"Why don't you ask Adan if he needs help in the owner's bath?"

Solana's cheeks turned rosy, and she dipped her head, but didn't protest. Instead, she marched across the yard. She said something to Adan, and he rubbed the top of her head, like he did with Braden. Ugh. He was so dense sometimes. Brisa would find a subtle way to clue him in to Solana's obvious interest later.

"Brisa!" Parker Quaid called her name.

She answered his question about the paint color for the trim versus the wall color. Then he carried the paint inside.

Dad gathered several cowboys to help demo the old porch and start building the new one. He had everything under control out front, so Brisa went inside.

Drake and Dylan had scored the drywall around both of the smaller bedrooms. Now they tapped holes in it with the blunt edge of a sledgehammer.

"You want to help?" Dylan asked.

She donned work gloves and safety glasses before she yanked back on the drywall with one hand while pressing against the score with her other. It snapped just like they had intended. It was kinda fun. Once they removed the drywall around the first doorway, Drake began framing the wider doorway under Robert's supervision.

Brisa and Dylan worked on the other doorway. His patient instruction warmed her heart. It helped that he looked handsome in his fitted t-shirt, flecks of drywall stuck in his dark hair. Her fingers itched to run through it, dislodging the debris. Instead, she grabbed the drywall putty.

Dylan measured the width of drywall needed, then jotted down the numbers on his phone. He grabbed a sheet of drywall and took it over to the sawhorses in the living room. He marked the sheet and cut it to size before bringing it back over to the new doorway. After securing it with a few screws, he ran the nail gun down the sheetrock over the studs. Brisa came behind him with the drywall tape and putty.

With the drywall in place, Brisa grabbed the light blue can of paint for Braden's room. He liked the color of the sky, but she thought it would be too bright for his room, so they had compromised on a lighter blue. Dylan placed drop cloths next to the wall to protect the carpet. He left and brought back two rollers and paint pans. They worked wordlessly on different walls in the small room. Even with her back turned toward him, she had been keenly aware of exactly where he was.

A loud stomach noise came from the adjacent wall. Brisa giggled and glanced at her watch. After one.

"I think your stomach is trying to tell us to break for lunch."

Dylan chuckled. "Yeah, I could probably eat two sandwiches at this point."

She turned toward him. "Why didn't you say something?"

"I thought we could finish this room first."

"Let's eat."

When she turned away from him, he lightly touched her arm. "Um, you've got something..."

He ran a finger along his own nose. Brisa rubbed the length of hers. He shook his head.

"Nope. Still there."

She tried again.

Laughter crinkled his eyes. "Let me."

He took a clean paint rag and dabbed it with the last of his water. Then he stepped so close she could practically hear his heart beating. Her mouth went dry as his fingers lightly angled her chin upwards. He ran the damp rag along her nose, applying more pressure when the first attempt failed. Then he turned her head one way before turning it the other.

"All clear." The husky timbre of his voice sent pleasant tingles over her skin. She cleared her throat.

"Let's go," she said, heading toward the fridge.

After she stretched her sore muscles, she retrieved two water bottles from the fridge. Brisa handed him one, then tilted hers toward him in a toast. "We make a good team."

Little lines formed at the edge of his eyes when his smile lit his face. "We do."

They stared at each other for a few seconds, causing her breath to catch. Attraction danced between them. Brisa wondered if maybe something deeper could develop between them. She thought she might like that.

A pang of guilt washed over her. She would have to give up Wrangler92 if she wanted to explore something with Dylan. It wasn't fair to either man. Yet she couldn't decide which man she liked more. Dylan had arranged all this for her and Braden. Not because he was friends with Adan. He knew she was a single mom with a disabled boy and he seemed interested, anyway.

Wrangler92 had several admirable qualities, too. Protectiveness, openness. He was so easy to talk to. The pinching in her gut gave her pause. If he was so easy to talk to, why hadn't she told him the truth about Braden?

The loud, bracing sound of a saw chewing through wood sounded repeatedly as men cut slats for the porch. They stepped over the threshold and hurried across the front yard.

Dylan offered her a lawn chair, and she sat while he picked up sandwiches from the food table for them. Would Wrangler do the same for her? She suspected he would. How could she have stumbled across two honest, noble men?

But did she really know Wrangler? He could be lying.

She hadn't met him in person yet. Maybe if she did, she could choose either him or Dylan without regrets.

She pushed the thoughts away and accepted the sandwich Dylan held out for her. As she chewed her sandwich, she allowed herself a moment to appreciate all that her friends and family were doing for her. She thanked God for them and their help.

Peace settled around her heart. If all went according to plan, she and Braden would move into the house the weekend before Thanksgiving.

9

ONCE BACK AT her parent's home, Brisa put Braden to bed. Then she sat in the quiet of her childhood room. When she opened the dating app, Wrangler's status showed as online. A smile flitted around the corner of her mouth as she typed out a message.

BRISA: *Hey there.*

WRANGLER92: *How did the remodeling go?*

Brisa blew out a breath. *Dylan, my brother's best friend, organized a bunch of volunteers from his family's ranch. I think there were twenty men between his brothers and hired hands. I can't believe he did this for me and my son.*

Too late, she realized her mistake. Her shoulders tensed and she held her breath as she watched the three little dots dance. The seconds ticked by as she waited for his reaction. Would he be angry she hadn't mentioned Braden before now?

WRANGLER92: *Do you have feelings for Dylan?*

Uh, oh. He was jealous. She swallowed down the regret. If she told him the truth, that would be the end of their conversation. If her having a son didn't turn him away.

BRISA: *I don't think so. He's my brother's best friend. We've known him for decades.*

The typing indicator flashed and faded. No message came. She waited a solid minute. Still nothing. His silence felt like torture.

BRISA: *I'm sorry I didn't tell you about my son Braden. Yes, I'm a single mom. He's four.*

The dots bounced while she held her breath again.

WRANGLER92: *I can see why you held that information back. From what you've said about your ex, I imagine you want to make sure anyone you talk to won't harm him.*

BRISA: *Exactly. I wanted to get to know you first. I thought we would have met by now, which is when I planned to tell you. But we've chatted for weeks. I should have mentioned him already. I hope that's not a deal breaker for you.*

Brisa bit her lip while she waited for his response.

WRANGLER92: *It's a surprise. Not a deal breaker, though.*

She deserved the curt answer, even if she hoped for something a little more reassuring.

WRANGLER92: *I'm sorry. I have to go. Send me pictures of the remodel. I'd love to see it. Sweet dreams.*

Wrangler's status flipped to gray.

She tried not to take the abrupt end to the conversation as rejection. He had asked for pictures of the remodel. And he wished her sweet dreams. Though he didn't wait for her to say the words back to him, like they normally did.

Why did the thought of losing him hurt so much? She never met him face-to-face. They had built their entire relationship through text messages in an app where they didn't even use their real names. He could be lying. His photo could be stock photography. He could be an axe murderer.

Ugh!

She didn't believe any of it. Something genuine came across in his words. That something drew her towards him.

Brisa placed her phone on her bedside charger. Then she readied herself for bed, hoping she might fall asleep quickly, despite the turmoil churning inside her.

DYLAN'S HEART LODGED in his throat. There was a disconnect between Brisa's dismissal of him in her text to Wrangler and how she reacted to him today. She had kissed his cheek, for goodness's sake. Blushed at his teasing while they worked together. Been sincerely grateful for his role in organizing the volunteers.

He's my brother's best friend.

The words hurt on so many levels. They felt like rejection *and* they were a reminder of his deception. His lies to Brisa. To Adan. Maybe he should bring everything out into the open with everyone. Tell her Wrangler92 was really Dylan Vargas. Tell Adan he wanted to date his little sister.

How had he ended up here—competing with himself for her affections?

Devon had tried to warn him something like this could happen. Unfortunately, he hadn't listened, even though he knew it was wrong.

Maybe it was time Wrangler92 met Brisa in real life. No more dual identity. No more sweet glances with her during the day and chats with his online alter ego at night. What a fine mess he had made for himself.

"You're frowning at your phone," Adan said from the other end of the couch. "Trouble in paradise?"

Dylan huffed. He couldn't exactly say he was jealous of himself. But Adan wouldn't let him ignore the question, either.

"Turns out she's a single mom."

"Is that a problem?"

Adan sat up straighter, and Dylan knew he was thinking about Brisa and how any guy might respond to her situation. He needed to tread carefully.

"No. I guess not. Just surprised me."

"When are you going to meet her?"

Dylan's shoulders raised and lowered with his loud exhale. "I'm kinda afraid to. What if she rejects me because of my stutter?"

That now familiar guilt punched his gut. He knew Brisa wouldn't reject him over his speech impediment. Certainly not after investing so much time to help him.

"Then she isn't worth your time. Have you told her about it?"

"No." Great. More guilt.

"Maybe you should."

Dylan frowned. If Wrangler92 told Brisa about his speech impediment, she would definitely put two and two together. How many men could have a stutter and work on one of the three guest ranches in the Wickenburg area and work with horses? Yeah, just the one. Him.

"I'm gonna turn in," he said before he hurried to his bunk, ending the conversation. He typed an apology for cutting the conversation with Brisa short, too. Then he closed out of the app.

As he laid there in the dark, the minutes ticked by slowly. He had to figure out how to meet Brisa without losing her. Or he just needed to let Wrangler92 disappear.

He could delete the profile. Except Brisa would believe the worst about the online version of him. She would think he was shallow, and he ditched her because she had a son. How awful that would feel. He couldn't do that to her.

It was impossible.

Dylan stuffed his arm under his pillow and tried to fall asleep, deferring the problem for another day.

10

"YOU LOOK DEEP in thought," River said as she took a seat across from Brisa.

Brisa set her phone aside and stirred her salad dressing into her salad. "I am. I think I have a problem."

"Nothing with Braden, I hope."

"Nothing like that."

Brisa expelled a loud breath and stabbed her salad with her fork. "I'm dating this guy online."

"Uh, oh. Not going good?"

"It's great. He's great. He's a wrangler at a local ranch. Works with his family and is a real upstanding guy."

River swallowed a bite of her salad. "So why the long stare when I came in?"

Brisa set her fork against the edge of the bowl and folded her arms on the tabletop, leaning forward. She glanced around. Drake busily filled customers' coffee orders at the espresso machine across the room. None of the cowboys stayed for lunch. A few ambled in to pick up box lunches and left. No Adan or Dylan either.

"I think I like two guys at the same time."

River's eyes widened, and she gasped. "Who?"

"Dylan and this Wrangler92."

River's lips stretched into a broad grin. "Dylan? Wow! Didn't see that coming."

"I know. Neither did I. We've had a few moments. Like

at the hayride a few weeks ago. And last week while remodeling my house."

"Really? What kind of 'moments'?"

"Like the ones you write about in your novels. You know, the chemistry zinging between the hero and the heroine. *The* stare."

River's face lit up. "With Dylan? Oh, how wonderful! He's such a great guy."

Brisa groaned, propping her chin on her palm. "I know. And if it were just him, that would be fine. Maybe. He is Adan's best friend and," she rolled her eyes, "that adds some complexity."

"But Wrangler92."

"I know! What am I gonna do?" Brisa stuffed a fork full of salad into her mouth, chewing forcefully. As if *that* would help her figure out the answer.

River glanced up and to the right. "Have you met Wrangler92?"

"Not yet. He wants to take things slow. Except last night, I think he might have been jealous about something I said about Dylan."

"Really? Sounds like he could have feelings for you."

"But we haven't even met yet." Brisa ate more of her salad as she waited for River's advice.

"What do you know about Wrangler?"

"Like I said, he's close to his family. Goes to cowboy church. Never kissed a woman. Works as a wrangler at a ranch in the area."

"Hmm. You know..." River's eyes rounded, and she set her fork down. "You don't suppose Wrangler is really Dylan, do you?"

"What?!" Brisa nearly choked on her water.

"Yeah, it sounds exactly like something I would write. A shy cowboy with a stutter dates a girl online, so he doesn't have to worry about embarrassing himself. Meanwhile, he gets to know her in person."

Brisa shook her head. "That's fiction. Stuff like that doesn't happen in real life." At least she didn't think it did.

"Think about it. Dylan is a wrangler. Works on his family's ranch—you don't get much closer than that. He hasn't dated, according to Dalton. He goes to a cowboy church. And he's been helping you with the remodel. He's always around."

Brisa pushed her salad away as her stomach churned. It was impossible. No way Dylan could be Wrangler, and vice versa. He wouldn't do that, would he?

"I don't know. Wrangler seemed pretty upset when I mentioned Dylan last night."

"What did you say?"

"I may have gushed a little about him organizing the volunteer day."

River grinned like the Cheshire Cat. "Then what?"

"He asked if I had feelings for him." Brisa's chest constricted. "And I said I don't know. That he was my brother's best friend. Our families knew each other for a long time."

"And if Dylan is Wrangler, how would you expect him to react to that?"

Brisa shook her head. Her voice was soft when she said, "They can't be the same."

River shrugged. "Why not keep talking with both? See where things lead."

MOVING DAY DAWNED bright and early. Brisa stretched, then she sprang from her bed. She took a quick shower before donning workout clothes. After pulling her hair into a ponytail, she gathered the last of her things and packed them.

Then she hurried downstairs. Mom agreed to watch Braden so he wouldn't be underfoot while Adan, Dylan, and

Derin moved her things into her new home.

"I'll pack the last of his things and bring them over this afternoon. Just text me when you're ready for him," Mom said before Brisa left.

She loaded the few boxes of things she had brought to her parents' house in the back of her Rav. Then she drove over to her storage unit. Derin, Dylan, and Adan stood leaning against Dylan's truck, waiting for her.

"Sorry, I didn't expect you already."

"We didn't want to be at it all day," Adan said, taking a swig of his coffee.

Dylan held out an iced coffee for her. "Cinnamon latte."

Heat warmed her cheeks. How he knew her favorite coffee, she did not know. She couldn't recall telling either Wrangler or Dylan about it. Maybe Drake. Yeah, Drake probably told him. Still, it was a kind gesture. She sipped the sweet beverage, grateful for the caffeine boost.

"Do you think two trucks and the trailer are enough space?" Derin asked.

Brisa scoffed. "The trailer alone is going to be plenty of space."

When her eyes darted to Dylan, she noticed his frown. Yeah, she knew it would shock them to see how little she owned. The house would feel huge and empty for a while. But she owned the bare necessities.

Dylan drove his truck with the trailer down the row of storage units. He parked the back of the trailer next to her unit.

She jumped out of his truck before any of the men opened the door for her. Her lack of possessions was embarrassing. She unlocked the unit and Adan shoved the door up, the metal slats clanging against each other loudly as it rolled overhead.

"That's it?" he asked.

"Um, hmm."

"Looks like one trip will do it."

Derin set the furniture mover on the ground and rolled it over to the unit. Dylan and Adan balanced her tallboy dresser against it and wheeled it into the trailer. Then two of them loaded her queen size bed frame, mattress, and box springs while the third one stacked several boxes on top of each other. Using the dolly, Derin transferred them to the trailer. The men loaded Braden's bedroom furniture next. Brisa grabbed the laundry basket full of empty hangers and set it in the back seat of the truck.

They loaded everything in just fifteen minutes. Then they used straps to hold it all in place so it wouldn't shift on the drive over.

Brisa drove her Rav in the lead, and they followed her over to the house. Derin continued on toward the ranch. She didn't blame him. Clearly, Dylan and Adan could manage her meager belongings.

DYLAN'S THROAT CONSTRICTED. When he and Adan talked about moving Brisa into her new house, he did not know it would take under two hours, including the driving time. She owned practically nothing.

"You okay with this?" he asked Adan.

He glanced over at his friend. Adan rubbed a hand on his jaw.

"I didn't know she needs furniture and probably a bunch of other stuff, too. She said nothing."

"Should we take her shopping?" Everything inside Dylan balked at the idea of walking away with Brisa still needing so much.

"Maybe she won't fuss if we go to the secondhand store."

Dylan shifted his truck into park and cut the engine. Then he dropped the trailer gate and started carrying things inside. The wheelchair ramp made it even easier to roll the dolly up the porch.

When Brisa tried to carry a box, he took it from her and used the dolly. "We've got this. You just tell us where everything goes."

"Thanks."

After thirty minutes, they had the trailer unloaded. Dylan stowed the furniture mover and dolly. When he entered the house, he heard Brisa and Adan arguing.

"Let us take you to a secondhand store. You need a couch. End tables. Something for the living room."

"I can't afford it, Adan. I barely have enough for groceries until payday."

Dylan frowned. He typed a group text to his mami, cousins, and River. They would take care of Brisa and not take no for an answer.

Adan finally convinced Brisa to go with them to look at used furniture. A tremendous victory. He would pitch in for the cost with Adan.

When he parked at the secondhand store, Brisa shoved the truck door open without waiting for either of them. Then she slammed it shut, the force rocking his truck. He kind of understood her frustration. She probably didn't want anyone thinking she couldn't take care of her son. It's not what he thought. Between what he had learned as Wrangler92 and from their conversations, he knew things had been hard with her ex. He figured she probably got rid of anything that reminded her of him.

He entered the store and walked toward the furniture section. Many of the items were in great shape. Dylan hung back and let Adan run the show. After twenty minutes, Adan convinced her to let him buy enough furniture for her living room.

Dylan picked out a table for four that he figured she would like. He paid for that and had it loaded by the time the store workers brought the rest of the furniture to the loading dock. He and Adan made quick work of loading and securing it.

"Do you need anything else while we're out?" Adan asked.

Brisa crossed her arms over her chest. "I'm fine, really."

Dylan caught Adan's attention in the rearview mirror. He shook his head slightly, and Adan let it go.

When they arrived back at her house, his mami, cousins, and sister-in-law stood on the front porch with arms full of grocery and household items. Perfect.

Dylan and Adan brought in the furniture. Then they headed back to the ranch for an afternoon of work. He rested easily, knowing the other women in his life would take care of the one he loved.

Mami texted him later in the afternoon to come over for supper. Just him. He couldn't recall a time where Mami had done something similar.

When he entered the house, Mami greeted him.

"Mijo!" She placed a kiss on each of Dylan's cheeks. "I love what you did for Brisa and that little niño. Come, we'll eat in the kitchen."

Dylan followed her through the massive living room. Brisa's entire house could fit in the room, he realized.

"Sit."

"Where is Papi? Dalton and River? Padre?"

"I sent them to the dining hall. I wanted to catch up with mi mijo."

Dylan's face heated.

"Will you bless the food?" she asked as she set a plate of street tacos, rice, and beans in front of him.

The fragrant spices brought nostalgic memories as his mouth watered. He bowed his head and prayed over the meal, eager to dig in to his mami's delicious food.

"Tell me, how are you doing?"

"Good." He ate one of the chicken street tacos, savoring the explosion of flavor.

"And how is Brisa?"

Dylan's shoulders sagged. "Poor."

"Mijo." Mami reached across the corner of the bar and placed a hand on his cheek. "You did well to text us."

"I... I like her, Mami."

"Si. I know. You have for a long time."

Dylan's eyebrows shot toward the ceiling.

Mami laughed. "I'm your mamicita. I know mi mijo's heart. You never could hide anything from me."

"I want to take care of her. Help her. Provide for her."

The truth of his words hit him square in his chest. He loved her. He had admitted it to himself already. But what he had just confessed to his mami scared him. He wanted to marry Brisa Franco. Remove all obstacles for her. Make sure she always had everything she needed and more.

Except he still hadn't told her he was Wrangler92. Until he did, such a future could not exist.

"I think she likes you, too."

Dylan's eyes jerked up to meet his mami's gaze. "Really?"

"Si. She's interested in you. And she sees you as father material."

"How can you know that?"

"The way she looks at you. Plus, she's a mami too. She wouldn't entertain a relationship with anyone she didn't think would be a good father. At least not anymore."

The conversation shifted to Mami's gardening and how much she loved her new daughter-in-law, River. When they finished eating, he stood and loaded the dishes into the dishwasher.

"Dylan, call Brisa and invite her and Braden to Thanksgiving here. I've already invited Harley and Heidi. Invite Adan, too, no?"

"Si, Mami. I will invite them."

"Gracias, mijo. I love you."

He kissed his mother on the cheek, just like he used to

94

do as a little boy when she read him bedtime stories. Then he headed back to the bunkhouse.

Before entering the building, he called Brisa, pacing the length of the porch. His boots clopped with each step while her phone rang.

"Hey, Dylan!"

Her cheerful greeting gave him courage. "Mami would like you and Braden to join us for Thanksgiving. She's already invited your parents. And I'll let Adan know."

"We would love to come. Can we bring anything?"

He could answer that without asking Mami. "No. Just yourselves."

"Alright. I'm looking forward to it."

"Me, too," he said before hanging up, realizing too late she probably heard that.

Because he couldn't leave well enough alone, he opened the dating app and asked how her day had been. They chatted for a while. After he wished her sweet dreams, guilt nagged him. He really ought to meet her. Tell her everything.

Or almost everything.

11

THANKSGIVING MORNING DAWNED. Dylan completed his morning chores in the stables, like every other day. There were no holidays for some things. Once he finished, he drove back to the bunkhouse and hurried through his shower. As soon as he was ready, he drove to the ranch house.

When he entered the house, an odd mix of aromas wafted. Pumpkin pie, apple cinnamon, and honey vanilla. The last was probably a batch of Mami's dessert empanadas or a candle. He sure hoped they were empanadas. What he didn't smell was turkey.

He poked his head in the kitchen, a potentially dangerous venture.

"Mijo!" Mami wiped her hands on her apron before she crossed the room and kissed his cheeks.

"How can I help?" Dylan asked.

"Ask your papi if he needs help with the tables."

He entered the dining room and found Papi counting chairs around the immense table.

"We might have enough space. Maybe," Papi muttered.

"How many do we have coming?" Dylan asked.

"All of us, Diego's family, Harley's family."

Dylan ticked off his fingers with each mention. "That's twenty-three."

Papi laughed. "Who do we put at the kids' table then? Besides Braden?"

"Adan."

"What about me?" Adan said as he joined them.

"We're short three spots, so you're sitting at the kids' table," Dylan teased.

"I feel like I should protest, but I don't mind hanging with my nephew. At least until I take off for a second meal."

"Two Thanksgiving dinners?" Padre chuckled in his gravelly voice. Dylan hadn't noticed the old man sitting in a chair.

"My girlfriend wants me to meet the parents."

"It's that serious?" Dylan asked.

"No. Not really. But I like her well enough to go."

"Adan, Dylan, can you get the folding table from the storage shed?" Papi asked.

Dylan nodded and Adan followed him, dodging the women in the kitchen on their way to the back door. When he opened it, the aroma of the smoker hit him. Dalton stood, taking the temperature on something.

"That smells good," Dylan said.

"Thought I'd try smoking a few turkeys."

"A few?" Adan asked.

"Mami loves the leftovers. If it turns out alright."

"Didn't you practice first?" Dylan asked, pondering the likelihood of ending up with food poisoning.

"Don't worry. I know what I'm doing."

Dylan sure hoped so as he opened the storage shed. He slid the dusty folding table out and leaned it against the side of the house. Adan showed up with a bowl of soapy water and a sponge. When he finished cleaning the table, he dumped the water in the side yard and helped Dylan carry it into the house. Once they set it up, Solana spread a plastic tablecloth over it. Papi tucked three chairs against it, leaving one side for Braden's wheelchair.

Before he knew it, the Francos arrived and Mami asked everyone to gather around the table for the prayer. Padre sat in a chair while everyone else stood. His grandfather looked exhausted, making Dylan wonder how many more holiday meals they would share with the patriarch of the family.

Papi asked everyone to hold hands for the prayer. Dylan glanced across the table as Brisa held her mother's hand on one side and his mami's on the other. Papi thanked God for all He had provided over the past year and for all He would provide in the coming year. Then he recited a beautiful verse about giving thanks to God. Mami let out a hum-sigh like she did whenever Papi or one of her sons did something that made her happy. Papi finished with a hearty "Amen" which they all echoed around the table. It was the one day of the year they did not recite the family motto. Papi had always said it was to focus on their gratitude instead of on their mission.

The scraping of chairs against the tile floor sounded as the family took their seats. Soon, conversation droned in the room. Dalton and River sat to his right and his other brothers sat to his left. Padre sat at the foot of the table, flanked by Renata on one side and Uncle Diego on the other, next to his wife, Aunt Katie. Then the Francos, Mami, and Papi sat at the head. Solana joined Adan at the kids' table with Braden. He thought it was nice that Adan gave Brisa the opportunity to join the main table.

"How do you like your new house, Brisa?" Mami asked. He loved the way her accent almost made two syllables out of the 'a' in Brisa's name.

"It's great. Thank you all for fixing it up. It was nice to move in and have it ready for Braden."

"I'll stop by and mow the lawn tomorrow," Dylan said.

"You don't have to do that."

"Nonsense!" Mami argued. "Let him sweat in the sun so you don't have to."

Heidi Franco laughed. "You said it, Catalina."

Brisa's cheeks turned rosy and Dylan dropped his gaze to the smoked turkey, which tasted delicious and was fully cooked. Mami promised she had double checked before serving it.

"Don't you have work to do?" Brisa asked.

Dylan shrugged. "I can spare the time."

She looked like she was about to say more when Mami asked Heidi a question about her Bible study in town.

Dylan focused on his food, glancing up often to watch Brisa. She wore her hair down in long waves. He loved how feminine it made her look. Her rust-colored dress heightened the deep blue of her eyes. She raised an eyebrow when she caught him staring.

Heat scalded his face as he swallowed the bite of food in his mouth. "That's a pretty dress."

"Oh. Thank you."

Dalton nudged his arm, and Dylan angled toward him.

"How is the new horse working out?"

"Thunder? I need more time with him."

"Dalton," Mami scolded. "No business on Thanksgiving."

"Sorry, Mami."

"Have you figured out when you are taking your honeymoon?" Papi asked.

It was Dalton's turn for a red face. "Not yet."

"Mijo, you need to spoil your *rio bonita*."

"We were thinking Maui," River interjected.

Dylan noticed she had placed her hand lightly on Dalton's leg, which seemed to calm his brother, killing whatever argument might have been brewing.

He wondered what it would be like to have Brisa at his side for a holiday meal. Would they whisper to each other? Trade secret looks or soft touches?

Maybe someday he would work up the courage to ask her out. Or he could just arrange for Wrangler92 to meet her. That felt safer. Easier.

When the meal finished and everyone complained about eating too much food, Derin and Devon took care of the dishes. The rest of the family and friends found a spot in the living room.

"Thanks for the delicious meal," Adan said. "I'm off."

Dylan wished his best friend a Happy Thanksgiving and told him he wanted the details on the date with his girlfriend later. Adan promised nothing.

Renata, Solana, and Heidi cajoled a few others into playing a board game. Dylan searched for Brisa and found her hesitating to join them, so he headed toward her.

"Want to take a walk?" he asked.

Brisa's eyes darted to her father. "Go. I'll watch Braden."

"Alright."

Dylan held back his grin until he opened the door and stepped onto the porch. It wasn't a date, but it was a step in the right direction.

As much as he wanted to hold her hand, they weren't there yet. He shoved his hands in his pockets and walked toward Mami's garden, Brisa next to him. He could get used to this.

BRISA SMILED AS she stepped onto the back porch. Dylan extended his hand, and she gently placed hers in his while she descended the stairs. A jolt of excitement raced up her arm, creating a liquid fire that spread throughout her body. The sound of her racing heartbeat filled her ears as she inhaled the scent of his cologne, a mix of cedarwood and musk. His touch was warm and firm, sending shivers down her spine. The energy between them was palpable.

As soon as her feet hit the ground, Dylan released her hand. He strolled beside her, hands in his pockets. The soft breeze carried the scent of fresh air, and the sun warmed her back, reminding her why she liked fall in Arizona. As they walked, she noticed the way his quiet strength made her feel safe—something she had desperately missed during her life with Tristin.

Brisa shuddered as they walked past his mom's garden toward a winding path, resolving to put thoughts of her ex out of her mind.

"He's a good boy," Dylan said, breaking the silence.

"Hmm. He is." God had blessed her with a resilient, jolly son.

"Can I ask? What happened?"

"A car accident." Her breath lodged in her throat as the old familiar guilt clenched her gut.

"Took his legs? And his father?"

Tears burned the back of her eyes. "Yes."

"I'm sorry for your loss."

Brisa stiffened. "The only loss I'm mourning is that of my son's future."

Dylan straightened. "Was your husband—"

She whirled to face him, her cheeks heating with anger. "He wasn't my husband," she said, her voice low and venomous. "And I don't want to talk about the vile man."

His eyes widened in shock, and he instinctively raised his hands in defense.

Her exhale was loud and deep, as if she were releasing all the stress and worries of her past. "Sorry. Tristin was not a good man."

When Dylan took a step forward again, she walked next to him along the path, the pea gravel crunching under the hard sole of his boots. The bright flowers in terracotta pots made it feel serene. As they strolled, the tension melted away from her shoulders.

"Sorry."

"No need to apologize. You don't have to tell me if you don't want to."

"It's fine. I met him two years after I moved to Phoenix. Things were…"

Brisa parsed her words. She liked Dylan and didn't want to scare him away with the worst of her baggage. Her lack of self-control and backbone embarrassed her.

"Intense. I had grown distant from God. When Tristin pressured me to move in, I... He had a way about him. I couldn't say no to him."

She stole a quick glance at Dylan, taking in the way his eyes studied her without a hint of judgment. His calm demeanor made her feel comfortable enough to continue speaking.

"The first six months were the best, and they weren't that great. When I got pregnant with Braden..."

The pregnancy had come as a surprise, but she had been happy about it. Tristin, however, had been anything but. He had accused her of trapping him, of trying to ruin his life, and had even threatened to leave her if she didn't get rid of the baby. She had tried to reason with him, to make him see they could make it work, but he had been unyielding. She could still see the fury on Tristin's face. The argument. The bruises on her arm.

Brisa cleared her throat. If only clearing the memories could be so easy.

"He had been very unhappy that I kept Braden."

Dylan stopped walking and turned to face her, holding her hands loosely in his. His thumbs stroked the back of her hands. Those chocolate brown eyes held so much compassion for her, despite what he had to be thinking. Her failures ought to cause him concern about her character.

"He made me pay for that decision over and over. When Braden was born, I knew I should have left. Only every time I tried, Tristin dragged us back."

Sometimes emotionally. Sometimes forcefully. She couldn't say it, though. Not to the decent, God-fearing man in front of her.

"Anyway. One afternoon, I had to work late. So I texted him to pick up Braden. I knew he'd be angry, but I didn't care. It should not have been a problem to ask a man to take care of his own son."

That horrible day rushed forward. A phone call from Tristin cursing her out. She had to hang up on him. Her client was waiting. She knew he would make her pay for it when she got home. The entire session with her client had her stomach in knots.

Then the call from the hospital. Her heart pounding in her chest as the words hit her like a ton of bricks. Tristin, her abuser, was dead. As the news left her feeling an odd combination of relief and numbness, the nurse's next words stole her breath, triggering a desperate need to get to the hospital as quickly as possible. Braden, her poor little boy, was in surgery, fighting for his life.

"He picked up Braden from daycare but didn't buckle him into his car seat."

Her voice cracked.

"Tristin had this bad habit. When he got angry, he drove aggressively. That day, he ran a red light, plowing into a minivan, killing a family of four. The impact..."

Tears soaked her cheeks. She wanted to look into Dylan's face, but shame kept her from doing so.

"The entire front end of his sports car crumpled. The impact killed him instantly. It had pinned Braden between the back of Tristin's seat and the backseat. His legs..."

A sob choked her. Dylan pulled her against his chest. The heat of his body provided comfort while his muscular arms encircled around her. His fingers caressed her loose hair. Slowly, she wrapped her arms around his middle.

"Crushed."

"Shh." Dylan's murmurs and gentle touch calmed her.

Brisa wasn't certain how long she cried against his chest, only that her tears drenched his shirt. When she finally leaned back, he tucked a knuckle under her chin, guiding her head up. As her eyes soaked in his loving gaze, he opened his hand, resting it lightly against her cheek. His sweet touch sent shivers down her spine. He failed to hide the depth of his feelings. She saw into his heart. This man couldn't love her already. And certainly not after what she had just told him.

She let her arms fall to her side as she stepped back. Dylan released his hold, though his eyes remained steady.

Embarrassment filled her as she swiped at the dampness on her face.

"Sorry about your shirt."

A smile tilted one corner of his mouth as he shrugged. Then he led them back toward the house.

"You're a wonderful mom, Brisa."

Her chest constricted. "How can you say that after everything I just told you?"

"He's happy. Despite everything."

Dylan's compliment oozed into the deepest cracks in her heart, bonding them together again like super glue. She had met no one who could make her feel so loved and cherished, and she knew she didn't deserve a man like Dylan. But she was determined to become a woman who could. She would work hard to be a better version of herself, one that he could be proud of. And maybe, just maybe, one day, she would be worthy of his love.

12

AFTER THEIR WALK, Dylan helped Brisa take Braden to her car. He wished she wouldn't run off, but he understood the emotional toll of talking about her ex and the accident. He waved as she drove down the lane, away from the ranch house, dust billowing up from her tires.

Holding her in his arms made him long for an actual relationship with her. No more secret identities. No more Wrangler92. Just Dylan Vargas.

He rested his hand over the damp spot on his shirt where she had cried on his shoulder. Everything in him wanted to provide for her permanently. More than a few random kind acts.

Dylan wiped his hand over his face. He didn't feel like going back inside to the noise of his family. So he texted Dalton they needed him at the stables. Yeah, he shouldn't have lied. But he couldn't handle Mami's questioning stare.

He climbed into his truck and drove over to the stables, parking in his usual spot. Then he entered the building, heading to his office. A box he hadn't noticed yesterday sat just inside. He looked at the return label. It was from the saddler. Braden's saddle had finally arrived. Perfect timing. Dylan had arranged for an equine therapy instructor to meet with him midweek the next week.

After digging his multi-tool from his pocket, he popped out a knife blade and sliced through the packing tape. The smell of leather filled his nostrils as he eased the specialized saddle from the box, styrofoam peanuts dropping onto the floor. He brushed off the remaining peanuts and tossed them in the empty box. Then he carried the saddle to the tack room. He snapped a picture and texted Adan, not expecting a response soon.

Dylan ran a hand along the seat. He studied the waist belt and the special stirrups. He remembered a video on the saddler's website, so he watched it. Seemed easy enough to figure out. If things worked out with the equine therapy instructor, he could have Braden in the saddle as early as next weekend. Wouldn't that be a wonderful surprise for both Brisa and Braden?

Since he was already in the stables, he set out fresh feed for the horses before driving over to the bunkhouse. Then he sat on the front porch in his favorite rocker and opened the dating app.

Happy Thanksgiving!

Surprisingly, Brisa texted back a greeting and told him about the meal with her family and friends.

WRANGLER92: *You back home?*

BRISA: *Yeah. Turkey makes me tired.*

Dylan smiled, remembering it did for most people. When she asked about his day, he told her that the saddle he bought for a friend came in. He hoped to give it to his friend next week.

So many questions came to mind, but he realized he could ask her none of them. She had never told Wrangler about her son's disability. She had said little about the accident, too. That was something she had only shared with Dylan.

It was getting harder and harder to navigate his interactions by text without revealing who he was. Maybe he ought to suggest they meet next weekend.

His thumbs hovered over the keyboard. At the last minute, he bailed on that thought. Soon, but not yet.

THURSDAY AFTERNOON, BRISA entered the arena. Dylan had asked her to meet him there. With Braden. Her stomach clenched. She hoped he would not put Braden on a horse.

Ever since the hayride, Braden talked about horses almost daily. He wanted to ride just like Uncle Adan and his best friend, Dylan. She couldn't deal with the disappointment it would cause her son.

She sighed as she wheeled Braden into the extensive building. A woman wearing jeans and a blue button-down shirt smiled at her. Her ivory cowboy hat shaded her eyes until she approached Brisa, hand extended.

"You must be Brisa and Braden."

Brisa coughed to mask her surprise before she accepted the woman's hand for a shake.

"I'm Lorissa Saunders. Dylan said you were coming."

"Sorry!" Dylan jogged up next to them, a little breathless. "Just got done with the vet."

He brushed his hands together, wiping away bits of hay. Dylan crouched in front of Braden.

"Lorissa is a certified equine therapist."

Brisa straightened her back. "Dylan, I don't—"

"She has over a decade of experience working with amputees. Teaching them how to ride horses."

Brisa's throat constricted as Lorissa led a palomino next to a platform in the arena.

"She's going to teach you to ride Miracle."

Brisa's eyes burned. "Dylan—"

"Relax, Bri," Adan said next to her. He slung an arm over her shoulders. "Lorissa is a pro. Dylan wouldn't have hired her if she wasn't."

When Dylan's gaze met hers, he raised an eyebrow. She knew he wanted her permission. Her lower lip quivered as she nodded in consent.

Adan hugged her to his side. "He'll be just fine, I promise."

Dylan wheeled Braden's chair onto the platform. Then he eased her son out of his chair and into a strange-looking saddle. Braden's face lit up with a huge grin.

"Don't make any sudden movements or loud noises," Dylan warned him. "Let me fasten you in."

Dylan reached around her son and buckled a belt into place. Then he adjusted the stirrups — at least that's what she figured they were — to match Braden's stumps. Then he stepped back and allowed Lorissa to walk Miracle around the arena. She spoke to Braden, though Brisa couldn't hear the conversation.

When Dylan came to her side, Adan dropped his arm.

"That's Braden's new saddle," Dylan said. "We'll keep it in the tack room, but it's available for him to use any time he wants, as long as Lorissa and Miracle are here."

"It works with the blades, too," Adan added.

"He doesn't have blades."

Adan's eyes remained locked on her son. "He does now."

Brisa followed his thumb as it hooked over his shoulder. On the bleachers sat a brand new pair of child-sized blades.

"Mom already had them fitted for him."

"What?!" Blades? A special saddle? An equine therapist? She couldn't believe this was happening.

"He used them for the first time yesterday."

Her tears spilled over and wet her cheeks. "You did this?"

Adan shook his head. "Dylan, me, Mom, and Dad all played a part."

"And we started a charity," Dylan said. "To fund an equine therapy program at Vargas Ranch."

"Healing Horses," Adan said. "Though we're not firm on that name yet."

Brisa's head turned from Adan to Dylan. She searched his eyes, and he held her gaze for a few heartbeats. She reached out and squeezed his hand.

At that moment, she finally understood the depth of Dylan's feelings for her. Beneath his quiet exterior, he cared for her. Possibly loved her. Why else would he do this? His eyes made it clear it wasn't because of his friendship with Adan.

"Mommy, look!"

Brisa turned her attention to the miracle before her, her son riding Miracle the horse, reins in his hand. He pressed against the horse's side with his stump while laying the reins across her neck same as an able-bodied rider. His eyes sparkled with life. His grin stretched from ear to ear.

She couldn't fathom how much this all cost. The saddle. The blades. An entire program, complete with an instructor.

"We're buying a few more trained horses over the next six months," Dylan said.

"And we've hired a CEO for the non-profit," Adan said. "She's already talking about a few smaller charity events early next year and a big rodeo hosted here next fall."

"Devon is organizing weekly riding lessons for the kids that stay here, so now Braden can join them," Adan said. "Just another kid learning to ride."

Brisa's shoulders shook as the sobs overtook her. Adan pulled her to his chest. She wrapped her arms around her older brother until her tears abated.

"All I've wanted since the accident is to give him the best. Let him be a kid. Do what other kids do."

"We know," Dylan said.

"It takes a village," Adan murmured.

Brisa wiped her hands on her wet cheeks. She turned toward Dylan and hugged him, too. "Thank you."

She couldn't be certain, but she thought he whispered, "Anything for you."

Braden's riding lesson lasted an hour. When he finished,

the four of them headed to the dining hall for supper before she headed home.

Even by bedtime, Braden still talked about riding the horse. She finally got him settled down for bed an hour late.

When she turned in for the night, she checked her phone. Wrangler92 had messaged her asking about her day. She couldn't bring herself to reply. Not tonight, after all Dylan had done for her.

Her conversation with River a few weeks ago came to mind. What if Wrangler92 was really Dylan Vargas? Was that even possible? Because if he wasn't, she might just have to let Wrangler go.

Brisa reached over and turned off her light as she tried to ignore the ache brought on by her thoughts.

DYLAN SIGHED AS he stared at the dating app. An hour ago, he had sent Brisa a message. No response.

Should that make him happy? Did it mean his gift of the saddle had the impact he hoped for? She certainly seemed pleased by the time they finished supper at the dining hall. Had it been enough to secure her heart for the real him?

He groaned. The entire situation with two versions of himself was out of control. He should have met her weeks ago. Now it felt twice as complicated. Between the walk after Thanksgiving dinner and the horse riding lessons, he sensed her pulling away from Wrangler92.

Was that a bad thing?

Maybe not. Maybe, just maybe, Brisa Franco was falling for him—the real Dylan Vargas.

But before he could ask her out as himself, he needed to know. Know if she had feelings for Wrangler. Know if she would still care for him, if she knew the truth.

He typed out his usual "sweet dreams" before closing

the app for the night. Then he went to bed.

By midnight, Dylan had been no closer to falling asleep than he had two hours ago. He stared at the dark ceiling.

Lord, I know I don't deserve your help here. Especially since I made this big mess. Please give me wisdom on how to untangle it.

His alarm blared through his foggy brain. Dylan reached over and turned it off. As he pushed off his bed and donned clothes, he had his answer. He must come clean. This weekend. No more delays. No more excuses.

After he poured a mug full of fresh coffee, he hopped into his truck and drove over to the stables. He went through the motions of caring for the horses. Then he hid in his office.

Dylan opened the dating app. Brisa never read his last message yesterday. What should he say now?

By lunch time, he was no closer to a decision. He hovered near the children's center, waiting for Devon to take a break. Glancing in the room, it looked like he was short staffed. Dejected, he shuffled out to his truck, returning to the stables.

At four, he finally worked up the courage to message Brisa.

I feel you are pulling away. If it's because we haven't met in person yet, I understand. I'd like to meet tomorrow night. At six at the steakhouse. He listed the cross streets. *Let me know if you'll be there.*

Dylan closed the app, knowing it would be a few hours before she responded. If she responded.

Around Braden's bedtime, a message finally came across the app.

Yes, I'll meet you. Bring a pink rose so I'll know it is you. Looking forward to it.

He replied he would be there.

This was it. Tomorrow would be his day of reckoning. He just hoped Brisa would still speak to him when it was all said and done.

13

SATURDAY AFTERNOON, DYLAN hefted a hay bale onto his shoulder and dropped it near Pansy's stall. Adan started at the opposite end of the alley. Dylan took advantage of the quiet as he slid the stall door open, spreading hay in the manger.

"Hey girl. Got a big date tonight."

He kept his voice low. As he filled the manger, he couldn't resist reaching out to caress her velvety nose.

"I've waited a very long time for this."

He took a deep breath in, the smell of hay and horse comforting. Maybe he should have waited until after his next session with Shirley before coming clean to Brisa. What if he totally froze?

A wave of unease washed over him, causing his stomach to coil. Pansy nudged his shoulder.

"Alright, girl. You're right. I'm overthinking it."

After refilling her water bucket, he gave her one last pat on her neck. Then he shut and latched the gate.

"I'll let you know how it goes in the morning."

A swish of her tail was the only response, bringing a smile to his face.

Next up was Caramel's stall. He greeted the calm mare with a few strokes along her neck, her favorite greeting. She leaned into his touch. A smile twitched at the corner of his mouth.

"What do you think?"

Her ears flicked back and forth, trying to understand his words. Dylan grabbed some hay and placed it in her manger.

"Do you think she'll be interested in me once she realizes I'm Wrangler92?"

Caramel stepped toward the manger and nibbled on her meal, hay crunching against her teeth. He rubbed a hand along her soft neck a few more times before he left her stall.

He continued the motions on down the line of stalls, talking to each horse as he fed them. The one-sided conversations helped him work through his anxiety while allowing him to bond more with the horses. The closer he came to Adan, he changed the topic to something he wouldn't mind his friend overhearing.

"All done?" Adan asked as he rubbed his back.

"Yup."

"Good. I've got a date tonight." Adan slapped his back.

"Same girl?"

Adan's gaze darted to a corner of the room. "Nope. Last one got weird when she found out I had been a rodeo star."

"Sorry, bro. Better luck tonight."

"You got any plans?"

Dylan shrugged, keeping up his secretive ruse. After tonight, Brisa would know the truth. It was only a matter of time before Adan found out.

As they walked down the alleyway for one last check, his stomach flipped and flopped. He checked his watch. Still plenty of time for a shower before driving into Wickenburg. He snagged his keys from his desk and flipped off the lights.

"Night everybody," he said to the horses. A few whickered, snorted, or stuck their heads over the gate as he passed by.

He drove over to the bunkhouse with the windows down. The cool evening air smelled fresh. Fresher than the odor wafting from him.

Once in the noisy bunkhouse, Dylan shaved again before jumping into a steamy shower. Then he toweled off and dressed in his Sunday best. His hand shook as he buttoned his blue starched shirt. He donned black jeans and dark brown boots. After fastening his brown belt, he added a dark brown cowboy hat to complete his outfit. Then he glanced at the pink rose from Mami's garden while he sprayed on cologne, the outdoorsy fragrance filling the air around his bunk. Surveying his appearance in the mirror, he felt confident. Mami would say he looked handsome.

Hopefully, his appearance would counteract any embarrassing stuttering or broken sentences. Dylan let out a sigh and headed toward the door. It was probably too much to hope.

"Hot date, big brother?" Derin teased as he lounged on his bed a few feet away, tablet propped on his lap, one earbud in. Probably watching football.

"Yeah."

Derin's eyes rounded as big as saucers, and he laid the tablet aside. "Really?"

Dylan nodded, scooped up the pink rose that Brisa asked him to bring, and turned on his heel, leaving his stunned brother behind. Before the door closed, he heard Derin ask, "Is he serious?"

A smile tilted up one side of his mouth. He had told no one about the date. Well, no humans. Certainly not his nosiest brother.

He climbed behind the wheel of his truck and backed out. As he transitioned from the dirt road to the paved highway, he felt the sudden rush of cool air from the open windows. He turned on the satellite radio, already on his favorite country station.

Lord, You know how much I like Brisa. Help me not to make a fool of myself tonight. Help her not to hate me for this.

Thirty minutes later, he pulled his truck into the parking lot of the steakhouse. He scanned the parked cars for her silver Rav4, hoping to glimpse Brisa. Of course, that might turn his resolve to jelly.

He sighed as he checked his appearance once more. Then he opened his truck door and swung his long legs out. After closing and arming his truck, he sauntered toward the entrance, rose in hand.

Then he saw her, and his pulse raced. Her blond hair fell in gentle waves over her shoulders. She wore braids to work, so he had rarely seen her hair loose. He liked it much better. The sleeveless green dress hugged her curves. Curves that hadn't been as obvious in her work uniform. His constricting throat threatened to cut off all the air in his lungs. Brisa Franco had dressed up for him—well, for Wrangler92. Maybe it would disappoint her to learn he was Wrangler.

He groaned. It was stupid to be jealous of himself. He just needed to explain the truth to her. Hopefully, she would understand and give him a chance.

Dylan's feet locked in place just outside the door as he watched her through the glass window. Her slender fingers brushed down the side of her skirt. Then they flew up to her golden locks and pulled them over her shoulder to one side before brushing them back again. Pink lip gloss caught the light, drawing his attention to the fullness of her lips.

Dylan swallowed. He was afraid that once he told her the truth, he would lose her forever. He wiped his sweaty palms down the leg of his jeans. There was still time to turn around and drive home. Save himself the rejection. Keeping him from a good throttling from his best friend.

But it was Brisa. The woman he had pined over for years, and had fallen madly in love with over the past few weeks. She deserved the truth from him. His pulse quickened as his fingers curled around the door handle.

Cowboy up, Dylan.

Squaring his shoulders, he eased the door open and flashed his best smile. Here went nothing. And everything.

BRISA FIDGETED WITH the skirt of her dress. Maybe she should have worn something less form fitting. The v-neck sleeveless dress was not too revealing. Modest and flattering. Still, she second guessed the dress. The color. Leaving her hair loose. Everything.

Ugh.

She resisted the temptation to pull her hair over her shoulder. Instead, she adjusted the strap of her brown saddlebag purse, which matched her strappy sandals.

Would Wrangler92 be everything she imagined? Did she even want him to be, now that she had fallen for the shy cowboy at Vargas Ranch?

As she argued with herself, Brisa's gaze landed on a pink rose in a tanned, masculine hand. Thick fingers clasped the delicate stem devoid of thorns. Her breath left in a whoosh as her eyes traveled up the muscular arm which pulled the top of the blue shirt sleeve taut. She noticed the fine black jeans, brown belt with a silver buckle polished to a sheen. Two-tone brown cowboy boots reflected the overhead lights. When her eyes finally settled on the man's face, she staggered back as if punched hard in the sternum.

"Dylan?" Her voice cracked.

It couldn't be. Her eyes had to be playing tricks on her. No way Wrangler92 and Dylan Vargas could not be one and the same.

She blinked and glanced back down at the pink rose. He extended the flower toward her, intense brown eyes begging her to take it, while remaining mute. She accepted the gift, confusion twisting her features and her heart.

Brisa studied Dylan's face, suddenly struck as mute as the man before her. Her mind struggled to reconcile the obvious truth. All those text conversations with Wrangler92 had really been with Dylan. Heat warmed her face as she remembered what she had said to Wrangler about Dylan. That had to have hurt him. She fanned herself with her hand as a wave of light-headedness caused her knees to go weak.

It couldn't be Dylan Vargas. No way.

He coughed. Then cleared his throat. Finally, her name escaped his lips in a hoarse whisper.

As a disturbing thought came to mind, she frowned and propped one hand on her hip.

"Is this some sort of twisted joke?" she asked, as anger pushed to the surface. "Did Adan put you up to this?"

The hurt in his eyes made her instantly regret her questions.

"N-n-no." His face pinched as he stumbled on the word, while his eyes darted between her and the door. He stood there, like a coiled spring, ready to make a break for it.

"Wrangler92," she said, his profile name from the dating app.

"M-m-me." He visibly swallowed, Adam's apple bobbing. His stutter, which she hadn't heard in weeks, proved just how anxious he was. He had to know she would be upset.

"Your table is ready," the hostess said, interrupting their awkward exchange.

After releasing a soft breath, Brisa flashed Dylan a tentative smile, despite her swirling emotions, remembering their peaceful meditations together. The countless acts of generosity from Dylan—a saddle for Braden. Helping with her house. Mowing her lawn. The bond her heart had formed. She swallowed down her anger, resolving to hear him out.

"Shall we?" she asked.

He placed his hand on the small of her back as she followed the hostess to their table. His cologne smelled woodsy and made her pulse race. Dylan held the chair for her and waited until she sat before taking the chair across from her. She laid the pink rose on the edge of the table.

Brisa laughed nervously as she accepted the menu, neck

muscles tensing. "How random is this? I guess we already know each other."

When her gaze connected with his, she stopped breathing for a moment. For a man who had said two stuttered words to her, his eyes shouted a very different message. Did he love her? He had recognized her when he responded to her post all those weeks ago and knew exactly who he was texting, didn't he?

"When you first reached out via the app, did you know it was me?"

He nodded.

Brisa rested a hand over her heart, trying to calm the butterflies dancing in her chest. Why would Dylan Vargas want to date her back then? He was her brother's best friend. Had hardly said a dozen words to her growing up. She had formed the impression that he was aloof and uninterested in engaging with others. Yet he connected with her online, knowing all about her disabled son and her return home after a decade.

"And you really wanted to date *me*?"

He reached for the water glass and downed a big gulp before answering. "For years."

The words settled over her heart in unexpected ways. Years. Him. One of the most reliable, honorable, family-loving men in the entire state. Her eyes burned, and she blinked the almost tears away. She had been suffering Tristin's abuse when a man like Dylan—Dylan himself—wanted to date her.

"You l-l-look," Dylan said. "Beautiful."

Good grief. Every word he said to her breathed life and hope into her battered, weary soul. Energy zinged between them, threatening to sear her heart. She needed to redirect the conversation before she lost complete control of her emotions.

"Everything you said on the app, that was really you? That was the truth?"

Those chocolate eyes pressed deep into her soul. It was like he could hear her thoughts before she spoke them.

"You've never dated? You won't kiss a woman until you love her?"

"Hi!"

Brisa jumped as a cheery server approached.

"My name is Alyssa. I'll be your server tonight."

She turned her attention to the overly peppy waitress. When Alyssa took their drink order, Brisa asked for an ice water with lemon. Dylan spat out the word "Coke," before the server bustled away.

Brisa folded the menu and slapped it down on the table. She couldn't decide if she wanted to end the date now or listen to his reason for waiting so long to tell her he was Wrangler92.

She had been through enough the last few years and she didn't need more drama. She wasn't sure if she could trust him, since he hid the truth for so long. Her thoughts and feelings jumbled until she forced the question most pressing on her heart out of her mouth.

"Why did you lie to me?"

14

DYLAN SWALLOWED HARD. Brisa had every right to be angry with him. He should have told her the truth before now. Somehow, he had to be honest without scaring her away.

"I."

His tongue stuck to the roof of his parched mouth. He closed his eyes. Maybe picturing a horse would help. Nope. The only thing he saw was Brisa's shocked face and her shapely body in that spectacular dress. He opened his eyes again.

As he set aside his menu, he leaned onto his forearms.

"Brisa, I have. W-w-wanted to. Ask you. Out for a long time."

Okay. A choppy sentence. It was a start.

"How long?"

Since senior prom. Not a good thing to say aloud.

"Does it matter?"

There. Redirect.

"But you recognized me?"

"Yes. I like w-w-what you wrote. Family values. A man who will w-w-wait for marriage."

Her cheeks blazed red and her eyes darted back to the menu.

Suddenly, doubt eked away his confidence.

"Did you mean what you wrote in your profile?" he

asked.

"Of course." Her voice rose in pitch.

"I am all... The things you asked for." He was. A man who loved his family. Was close to them. Chivalrous. Anything less than that and Mami would have his hide.

Alyssa set their drinks on the table and hovered with her pen poised over her notepad.

"One minute, p-p-please?" he asked as heat crawled up his neck and over his face.

The lively server nodded and promised to be back in a few minutes.

"If you want to leave, I'll understand." The words came out smoother, but twisted a knife in his heart.

Her blue eyes—so gorgeous—held his gaze for a moment. He felt every heart beat as loud as thunder while he waited. Then she wilted against the back of the chair.

"Why not just talk to me, Dylan? Ask me out instead of this ruse?"

"My stutter. It was so easy to talk to you on the app. To let you see me without my..." He sucked in a loud breath. "Without my speech impediment getting in the way."

He wanted to take her hand or touch her arm. Something to reassure her. But he held back.

Brisa took a sip of her water with lemon. A frown settled on her brow. "What did I do to make you think I would be so shallow?"

Bubbly Alyssa returned and took their orders before flitting away like a hummingbird, stopping for a quick check-in at her other tables.

"Brisa, I don't think you are shallow. Never have. Others have treated me differently my entire life. I let my fear have a foothold when I should have told you the truth immediately."

Her lovely blue eyes rimmed with red. He saw the hurt in them. Hurt he had caused by not being honest with her. He prayed she would forgive him. That he wouldn't lose her.

Her lips parted as if she planned to say more when Alyssa arrived with their entrees.

Dylan reached across the table for Brisa's hand. When her soft, lithe fingers wrapped around his rough ones, heat rushed up his arm all the way to his heart.

"Shall I pray?"

At her nod, he said a brief prayer for the food and their conversation. When he finished, her hand lingered on his for a few seconds. Dare he hope she might actually forgive him?

Once she swallowed a bite of salad, she finally spoke.

"I think I understand why you wanted to text. Though I'm not saying I'm ready to forgive you yet."

"Fair enough."

Brisa swallowed another bite of food. Then she sighed.

"You could have saved me countless hours of worry, you know."

Dylan's heart rammed against his chest as he forced his voice to sound light. "Oh?"

"Yeah. I fell for Wrangler92 as much as I fell for you."

He rested his silverware on the edge of his plate. Was she saying what he thought she was saying?

She smiled at him, and he breathed again.

"Yes, Dylan Vargas, I like you. A lot. And I like Wrangler92 a lot. And..." She lowered her gaze to her plate before she looked up at him through her lashes. "I'm really glad they are the same man."

He squeezed her hand as her words healed a broken place in his heart.

"Are you going to eat before your food gets cold?" she teased.

Seemed like she was ready to move forward. He breathed easier as he picked up his silverware. Then he cut off a bite of his nearly mooing steak. Perfect.

"Rare, huh?" she asked as she scrunched her nose. "I prefer mine more on the medium-well side."

He winked at her as he swallowed the tender morsel. "You miss all the flavor that way."

She snorted. "And food-borne illnesses."

Dylan laughed. "Haven't gotten sick from steak yet."

"There's that pesky little word. 'Yet.'"

She popped a bite of her steak into her mouth. When she closed her eyes and hummed, he chewed slower, pulse skittering. Brisa was all woman. Feminine and soft. More beautiful than a glorious Arizona sunset. And she liked him. A lot. Her eyes flew open, and his face heated as he looked away.

Throughout the rest of the meal, they fell into the normal rhythm of conversation, giving him hope they could become a couple.

When they finished their entrees, Brisa declined dessert, so he skipped it too. Then he held her chair for her and offered his arm as they wove between the tables. He pushed the doors open and the cool temperatures caused him to shiver as he walked her to her car.

Brisa paused with her back toward her driver's side door. She looked up at him with those lake-blue eyes. Dylan's breath shallowed and his pulse raced. He had to see her again soon, now that there were no more secrets between them.

"Thank you—"

"Would you—"

They spoke at the same time. He dipped his chin, allowing her to go first.

"Thank you for the lovely meal and for telling me the hard truth."

"You're welcome." He took her hands in his. "W-w-would…"

Brisa reached up and placed a hand on his cheek. Tingles traveled from her touch all the way to his heart. "It's me, Dylan. Brisa. No need to be nervous."

He could think of one thousand reasons to be nervous. One of those included fearing what Adan might do when he found out Dylan had been online dating his little sister.

"Would you go on a horse ride with me next Saturday afternoon?"

"Let me get back to you. I need to… Can I let you know in a few days?"

Dylan nodded, hoping she would say yes soon.

The silence stretched between them as her eyes studied his. She leaned forward slightly and his heart nearly stopped. He had never kissed a woman. He had meant what he told her as Wrangler92 — that he wouldn't kiss a woman unless he loved her.

His breath stuck in his throat as he considered it. He was pretty sure she wanted him to.

BRISA COULD BARELY inhale without savoring Dylan's woodsy cologne. It stirred her senses and drew her toward him. She loved him — both the flesh and blood man and the soul he shared with her online. Her eyes locked onto his for a few heartbeats before she leaned in slightly. Then her gaze dropped to his lips.

When his hand cupped the side of her face, she closed her eyes. His light touch stirred the butterflies in her stomach. Several seconds passed and nothing happened, driving her nearly insane with anticipation. Then his thumb brushed softly across her lips.

"I will not kiss you, Brisa."

Her eyes flew open, and she furrowed her brow, trying to hide the hurt churning inside of her. After all that, did he not love her?

"I want to. But not on the first date." His husky timbre punctuated the desire reflected in his eyes.

Oh. Maybe he loved her but wanted to go slow, still. She should have expected it when she asked for a chivalrous man. She blew out a shaky breath as his hand moved to open her car door.

"See you at church tomorrow?" he asked as he maneuvered the door between them.

"Yes."

When he held out his hand, she placed hers in it before she slid behind the wheel. Then he squeezed it lightly before releasing it, leaving behind a trail of warmth wriggling up her arm.

"Sweet dreams, Brisa."

Then he closed the door before she could respond. He moved out of her way, still standing nearby as she pulled out of the parking spot. He waved as she drove away. Glancing in her rearview mirror, she caught his grin right before he stuffed his hands in his pockets and casually strolled toward his truck. She held a hand over the cheek he had touched for a few seconds before focusing on the drive home.

By the time she arrived, Brisa wondered how she would ever fall asleep that night. She was so relieved that he and Wrangler92 were the same man because she never would have been able to choose between them.

When she opened the door to her house, Mom and Dad looked up from the TV.

"Home already? We just put Braden down a few minutes ago," Mom said.

"He's probably still awake," Dad added.

Brisa thanked them and hurried to her son's room. She stood in the doorway for a moment, letting her eyes adjust to his nightlight.

"Mommy?" His sweet, drowsy voice always tugged on her heart.

She nudged the door open and sat on the edge of the bed. "Hey, cowpoke."

A soft smile spread across his face as he closed his eyes again. "Night, Mommy."

Brisa leaned down and placed a kiss on his cheek. "Sleep well."

When she entered the living room, Dad turned off the TV.

"Did you have a good time?" Mom asked.

Brisa smiled. "Yes. He was a perfect gentleman."

Dad stood and kissed her on the top of her head. "I'm glad."

Then he excused himself to clean up her kitchen.

"You'll never guess who he is," Brisa said.

"Someone we know?"

Brisa nodded before blurting out, "Dylan Vargas."

Mom's eyes rounded. "Oh, my! He's such a fine young man. Little quiet, but good to the core."

"I know."

A smile stretched across Mom's mouth. "And you like him."

Brisa's cheeks warmed. "Very much."

Then she cleared her throat. "What do you think Adan will do?"

Mom frowned. "He better not *do* anything besides be happy for his little sister and his friend. It's none of his business who you date."

Brisa hoped that was true, but she couldn't shake the feeling that Adan might not be as supportive as Mom expected.

"Did he kiss you?"

"Mom!" Brisa's cheeks burned. "Not on the first date."

Mom's grin returned. "So there will be a second?"

"I think so. He asked me to go riding with him next Saturday."

"You should go. We can watch Braden. He's such a good little boy."

Her eyes burned with relief. "Thanks Mom."

When Dad finished cleaning up the kitchen, Mom stood.

"I'm so happy for you, Bri. He's a good man."

Brisa hugged her parents before they left. Then she padded toward her bedroom, phone in hand. She scrolled to Dylan's contact. She had taken a picture of him at Thanksgiving when he wasn't looking and his joyful smile stared back at her. Dylan, her sweet, shy cowboy. She tapped on the picture and started a text message.

Sweet dreams, my wrangler. She added a blowing-kisses emoji to the end and tapped send.

That should reassure him she wanted to pursue a relationship with him. Wait, did that mean Dylan Vargas was officially her boyfriend now?

A smile stretched across her face as she snuggled deep into her bed and turned out the light. Sweet dreams indeed.

15

DYLAN SMILED AS he climbed behind the wheel of his truck. Brisa wanted him to kiss her. She had even been a little disappointed he hadn't. He didn't regret the decision. It was the right thing. Especially since he had the long game in mind. Not some fleeting rush of feelings that would burn out in a year. He wanted a lifetime.

With that as his goal, he needed to take his time with her, especially after hiding the truth from her.

As he cut the engine, he slid out of his truck, whistling his way to the bunkhouse. The starry night sky rejuvenated him as much as thinking about his evening with Brisa.

His phone pinged. Not the dating app, but a text message. Brisa wished him sweet dreams. He typed the same back to her, even though he had said it before they left the restaurant parking lot.

Dylan straightened his shoulders and opened the bunkhouse door. He ducked inside, glancing toward the commotion in the living room. Derin, Devon, and Drake yelled at the TV along with Parker and a few other cowboys. A loud groan erupted.

"He dropped the ball!" Derin hollered. "Hold it like a baby!"

A smile twitched at the corner of his mouth. Football.

"Hey, Dyl," Devon greeted him. His brother shuffled toward him.

"Where you been? We saved you some pizza."

Dylan jerked his head toward their private bunks, and Devon followed him.

"I finally told her."

"Brisa?"

Dylan nodded, a grin splitting his face.

"And she's okay?"

"She's relieved. She said she was falling for both versions of me."

"Oh, wow." Devon rubbed a hand over his face. "Wow. Um. Wow."

Dylan set his hat on its hook and toed off his boots.

"Does Adan know?"

Dylan spun to face his brother. "No. And you can't tell him. I'm s-s-serious. Tell no one."

Devon shook his head. "I won't. But isn't he kinda over-protective?"

Dylan swallowed, trying to moisten his sticky mouth. "We aren't kids in high school. We're adults."

The argument sounded weak to his own ears, and he doubted Adan would be okay with it. But it was Brisa. She wanted him to kiss her. They had a connection. At long last, there were no secrets between them. He could explore a relationship with her. He wouldn't let Adan stop it, no matter their long-standing friendship.

"Wow. Was it a good date?"

"Date?" Derin's voice came from the doorway. "Dylan went on a date?"

"Talk later," he said to Devon. Then he turned toward the doorway to see a dozen cowboys looking his way, including his brothers, Derin and Drake.

Dylan sat on the edge of his bunk and unbuttoned his dress shirt. He stood to hang it back on a hanger in his closet.

"Did you go on a date?" Drake asked, eyes full of mirth.

"Yes."

"With who?" Derin asked.

Devon cleared his throat. "A woman."

Dylan narrowed his eyes. Devon pursed his lips.

"I met her online."

Derin laughed. "Online? Who knew?"

"Come on, Der. Leave off it," Devon warned.

"No. This is impossible to believe. Dylan has never dated. Never. So why the sudden urge to date online?"

Dylan rose to his full six foot four inches. He walked toward Derin, standing toe to toe. Though Derin's shoulders spanned several inches wider than his own, Dylan could take his younger brother. He hoped.

"W-w-what's it to you?"

Derin laughed and shook his head. "I don't believe it."

"Derin, stop." Drake grabbed his arm, but Derin shook it off.

"It's my fault," Adan's voice came from the back of the crowd. "I put an app on his phone."

Adan pushed through the crowd and clamped a hand down on Dylan's shoulder. "It was an excellent date?"

Dylan nodded, keeping his eyes locked on his annoying brother's.

"Good. Let's not ruin the night with blows, then."

Drake nudged Derin back while Adan moved in front of Dylan.

"Wanna tell me about it?"

"I don't kiss and tell."

"Not asking you to, bro. Just offering an ear to listen."

"How was your date?" Dylan asked, redirecting Adan to his favorite subject: himself.

While Adan regaled him with antics from his mediocre internet date, Dylan changed into shorts and a t-shirt.

Devon slouched on his bunk nearby, his eyes never leaving Dylan. Maybe it had been a mistake to tell him about Brisa. He could feel Devon's unanswered questions. The main one was probably the same as his own. How would

Adan react when he told him?

THE NEXT MORNING, Dylan rose before the sun, still in a good mood. He donned a pair of jeans, a snap front shirt, boots, and hat. He and Adan stepped into the common area at the same time.

"Coffee?" Adan asked as he started a fresh pot.

They waited in silence for the brew. Then they each poured a travel mug full before they climbed into Adan's truck.

"You said little about your date last night," Adan said as he backed out of his parking spot. "Was she pretty?"

Dylan took a swig of the black brew, stalling. He should have figured Adan wouldn't let it go.

"Beautiful. Perfect smile."

Adan chuckled. "And?"

"And what?"

"You gonna see her again?"

Dylan drank another gulp of coffee.

"Uh, oh. I'm sorry, Dyl. I misunderstood. I thought you said it was a good date."

"It was. I invited her riding." He brushed at some dirt on his jeans. There was no way he could keep this a secret for long.

"Congrats."

Adan didn't ask anymore questions while they fed, watered, and turned out the horses before going back to the bunkhouse to shower and dress for cowboy church.

Dylan didn't normally wear cologne for church, but opted to in the hopes he might see Brisa at church. Then he rode over with Devon.

At church, he greeted his parents, Padre, Dalton, and River before shuffling into his seat. As the music started, he caught sight of Brisa wheeling her son to the end of the row where the Franco family sat. Adan grabbed the chair on the end and moved it out of the way before he sat next to his mother. Brisa wheeled her son into the empty spot.

As Dylan tried to focus on the music, shame filled his heart. How many things did he take for granted every day, like sitting in a chair or not having to worry about making room for a wheelchair. Yet Brisa dealt with it daily. He wanted so badly to help her.

Devon nudged him and he faced forward again, singing the words softly, though keenly aware of Brisa several rows away.

Yeah, he wasn't gonna be able to keep his secret from Adan much longer.

BRISA MOUTHED A "thank you" to Adan for moving a chair out of the way for Braden. She locked the wheels before she faced forward. As her eyes landed on the Vargases, she caught Dylan's profile. He had seen her.

She pushed the thoughts of him out of her mind as she sang the familiar worship song. When the pastor took the podium, Braden squirmed.

"I have to pee."

Heat warmed her cheeks at her son's overly loud whisper. Half the congregation must have heard. To the pastor's credit, he didn't skip a beat.

Adan stood. His eyes went wide, but he motioned for her to stay seated. She shook her head. He did not know how to help her son.

"I got this, Bri," he hissed, unlocking the wheels, and guided her son out of the sanctuary.

Brisa glanced at her watch. If they weren't back in ten minutes, she would check on them. She focused on the pastor's message about the new self. It spoke to the broken areas of her soul. God had changed her from who she had been when she was with Tristin. She was new. Clean.

Finally, Adan returned with her son. She did not know how long they had been gone.

Dylan approached as soon as the service ended. Brisa smiled at him.

"Morning," Dylan said, his eyes holding her gaze for several seconds.

"Morning," she whispered shyly.

"Something going on between you two?"

Judging by the annoyance in Adan's tone, she presumed Dylan had not told him they were dating.

"Brisa!" Catalina broke the tense moment by pushing her way past Dylan to swallow her in a welcoming embrace.

"It's good to see you."

While Catalina spoke with Braden, Brisa turned to Adan and caught him glaring at Dylan. She hoped she hadn't just come between the two friends.

"Brisa, join us for lunch at the ranch house?" Catalina asked. "Your parents have already agreed. Adan, we'd love to have you too."

"Wouldn't miss it."

Brisa caught the warning in Adan's tone, probably intended for Dylan. She held back a sigh. He had no reason to be upset. She could date who she wanted.

"I can ride with you," Dylan said to her. "I rode over with Devon."

"Give us a minute, sis," Adan ground out the words through gritted teeth.

Brisa wheeled Braden out to her car, praying Adan would go easy on Dylan.

16

"WHO HAVE YOU been dating online?"

Dylan glanced away, pretty sure he didn't have to confirm Adan's suspicion with words.

Adan stood with fists propped on his hips, feet apart, back ramrod straight. Darkness clouded his eyes. When Dylan tried to dodge him, Adan grabbed his arm.

"Where do you think you're going?" Adan growled, his grip tightening on Dylan's arm. "You think you can just walk away from this?"

Dylan winced in pain but didn't back down. "You're overreacting."

Adan's eyes blazed with anger. "Overreacting?" he spat. "She's my little sister!"

Dylan jerked his head toward the door. Adan followed him outside, and they rounded the church to the deserted side lot.

"She may be your younger sister, but she's an adult. She can ch-ch-choose to date whomever she wants."

Adan fisted Dylan's shirt in his hands and slammed his back against the side of the building. "You lied to me. You knew I wouldn't like this, and you lied."

Dylan circled his arms up and over Adan's, bringing them down hard enough to force Adan to release his shirt. "I don't want to fight with you."

"How long did you know it was Brisa?"

"From the moment I responded to her profile."

Fury marched across Adan's face, followed by a flicker of betrayal. Dylan swallowed down his own anger as he crossed his arms over his chest. He expected Adan to be mad. To feel some measure of betrayal. He just hoped they could work it out.

"I can't believe you. We've been friends for... For a lifetime. I stuck by your side all these years and this is how you repay me?"

"I've loved Brisa for a long time."

Adan leaned forward, shoving his palm hard against Dylan's shoulder. "You don't even know her. You don't know what she's been through."

"She told me everything. And I love her. And I think she might love me."

Dylan's head jerked back as Adan's fist connected with his jaw. Pain radiated from the spot, followed by heat. Light swirled around him as he shook it off. He hadn't seen that coming.

"We're done," Adan spewed the words through gritted teeth before storming away.

Dylan rubbed a hand over his jaw as he worked it from side to side. He probably deserved some of Adan's anger for not telling him from the beginning. But Dylan was right that Brisa could make up her own mind. She already had. And it was none of Adan's business who Brisa dated. Or who Dylan dated. Still, the guilt gnawed at his gut as he jogged out to Brisa's car.

"Here, let me get that," he said, reaching for the collapsed wheelchair.

She stepped aside, and he stowed it in the trunk. Then she took a small step toward him. On tiptoes, she leaned in and placed a feather-light kiss on his cheek. The scent of her sweet perfume filled his nostrils, and he felt the warmth of her breath on his skin. As she spun away, her dress swished gently, and he heard the soft rustle of the fabric. It all happened so quickly that he wondered if he had just imagined it.

"You coming?" she asked.

He stirred before closing the trunk. Then he hopped in the passenger seat as she cranked the engine and pulled out of the church parking lot.

"Sorry about Adan. I can talk to him later."

"We'll work it out." He hoped.

"I guess he's not coming to dinner?"

Dylan shrugged as she turned onto the lane toward the ranch house.

"I'd still like to go for that ride next weekend. Mom said she'd watch Braden."

Despite his concern over the state of his friendship with Adan, his heart soared over her news. She wanted to go for that horse ride. With him. Perhaps she really had forgiven him last night. It sure seemed like it.

When she parked the car and opened the trunk, he headed to the back to retrieve the wheelchair. He made quick work of setting it up and wheeling it to the side of her SUV. Once Braden sat securely in it, he carried the boy, chair and all, up the few porch stairs, his boots thudding loudly. Brisa thanked him as she held the door open.

"Smells good in here," Brisa said.

"Dalton must have smoked something this morning."

Just then, his older brother entered the kitchen from the back door with a tray of mouthwatering meat.

"I put a few briskets in overnight."

Dylan showed Brisa and Braden to the huge dining room table before he returned to the kitchen. When he asked how he could help, Mami shooed him away. "Vamos. Spend time with Brisa."

When he entered the dining room, he sat across from Brisa. Before he said anything, the rest of his family gathered around the table.

Papi cleared his throat and led the group in a prayer.

Once he finished, silverware clanked against serving trays as they passed the food around the table. The smoky aroma of brisket, ribs, and pulled pork filled the room. Dalton had cooked the mac n cheese in the smoker too, causing Dylan's mouth to water. He couldn't recall Padre ever doing that. The low buzz of conversation brought comfort to his soul. He loved his big, noisy family and neighbors.

Brisa ducked her head for a few seconds. A soft smile stretched across her face. Then she looked Dylan in the eye, causing his heart to speed up. Yeah, she forgave him for his dual identity.

That horse ride couldn't come soon enough. He already had the perfect spot in mind to tell her of his undying love. To kiss her if she returned his feelings. He could hardly wait.

Catalina eyed Brisa when the meal started. Then she glanced at her son.

"Are you dating?" Catalina asked Dylan.

He grinned. "Yes, Mamacita. The son you thought might never marry is dating Brisa Franco."

Brisa's face heated as Catalina hugged her first, quickly followed by her mom.

"We're so happy for you," Tres said.

Mom and Dad echoed the sentiment. So did River and Dalton before Dylan's younger brothers congratulated him. Derin didn't look overly convincing, but he could be surly sometimes.

"What's dating, Mommy?"

Brisa's eyes widened, and she looked at her mom, questions in her eyes. How could she explain dating to a four-year-old?

"Um. When two people really like each other and they want to figure out if they want to get married, they date."

Dad laughed. "I'm not so sure he'll understand that, either."

"Did Grandpa and Grandma date?"

"Yes, honey," Mom said. "Grandpa dated me. When we decided we wanted to spend the rest of our lives together, we got married."

Braden frowned. "Oh."

Brisa's heart lodged in her throat as she watched her son process that information.

"Like Mommy and Daddy before Daddy died?"

She closed her eyes as her face burned. How could she explain that to him?

"Kinda," Dylan said.

Braden crossed his arms over his chest. "I don't want you to be mean."

Dylan coughed, and Brisa knew she needed to set her son straight.

"Baby, Dylan will not become mean."

"But Daddy was. I don't miss him."

Neither did she, but she figured that would not be appropriate to say. "Your daddy was very different from Dylan. You're right. He was mean. And angry. And he hurt us a lot. But Dylan isn't anything like your daddy. Just like Grandpa and Adan aren't."

"But you aren't dating Grandpa or Uncle Adan."

She sighed, trying to mask her frustration. "No, I'm not. What I'm trying to say is that, just like Grandpa and Adan are good men, so is Dylan."

"Oh! Like Superman is good?"

"Yes."

"And Daddy was bad?"

"Yes."

"'Kay."

Braden uncrossed his arms and started eating again. Guess she had explained good enough for him.

After supper, Dylan followed her home, and they spent

the afternoon watching movies with Braden and chowing down a gigantic bowl of popcorn. Perfect second date.

When Dylan left after the second movie, Brisa picked up her phone and dialed Adan. Voicemail. Great.

"Adan, you're being a jerk," Brisa said, before hanging up. Then she texted him the same.

BRISA: *You're really going to blow up a twenty-plus-year friendship because of me?*

ADAN: *He lied.*

Brisa rolled her eyes. *Yes, he deceived us. I've forgiven him. Can't you?*

ADAN: *Butt out, sis.*

Ugh.

As much as Brisa wanted to fix their friendship, Adan was right. She needed to step out of it. The two of them needed to navigate it without her interference.

BRISA: *Even though you're angry with him, I hope you can be happy for me. He's a million times better than Tristin.*

She breathed in deeply and let it out slowly. *I could see a future with him. I hope you'll be in our future too.*

There. She had said what she needed to. Now she could let it go.

17

THE NEXT FRIDAY morning, Dylan could hardly contain his excitement about his ride with Brisa tomorrow. Just one more full day of work to get through first.

As he placed the bridle on Thunder, he noticed the horse seemed antsy. Thunder could sense his excitement, so he took a few calming breaths. He spoke in soothing tones and offered him a piece of sliced apple, his favorite treat. Once he secured the bridle, he shoved open the gate and guided the horse down the alleyway to groom him. Then he saddled the dark brown horse and led him out of the barn.

The light glinted off the windshield of the row of pickup trucks in the parking lot. Dylan slid his sunglasses on. Thunder side stepped, pulling the lead taut.

"Easy boy. Whoa."

Instead of mounting the horse as he originally planned, he took him to the corral. As he walked the magnificent stallion around, the beast settled down. Wonder what spooked him. Maybe the glare from the truck windows?

Dylan tried to recall the notes from the previous owners. They hadn't disclosed problems with Thunder, but that meant nothing. Wouldn't be the first time he discovered a quirk or issue with a horse after purchasing it. He could work with any horse.

He looped the reins over the corral fence and texted Adan he was riding out with Thunder. Planned to ride the northern boundary line before cutting back by the base of Dalton Peak toward the barn. Even though Adan still wasn't speaking to him, he knew Adan would alert others if he didn't show up when expected.

Dylan loosened the reins and climbed into the saddle. He leaned down, rubbing Thunder's neck. The raw power beneath him never failed to amaze him.

"Let's go."

He urged Thunder forward at a gentle walk along the horse trail skirting the resort. As they left behind the busy part of the property, he eased Thunder into a trot. The horse tossed his head before settling into a steady pace. With the northern fence in sight, he squeezed the horse's sides and leaned forward, ready for the canter. Thunder answered to his expectations, no fussing this time. After a few minutes, he hunched over and let Thunder have his head.

The horse galloped smoothly, covering the terrain quickly. Dylan's breathing remained steady, and he felt the press of Thunder's lungs against his legs. His black mane whipped in the breeze created by the fast movement. Dylan's abs burned with the effort to control his own.

As Dalton Peak loomed larger, he slowed Thunder to a trot, then a walk. Both man and beast breathed the heavy sighs of a satisfied run.

Thunder seemed calmer now, after the vigorous exercise. Dylan would enjoy riding him. He was too feisty for inexperienced tourists on a trail ride. Eventually, he needed to determine how the horse worked around cattle, since that was why he bought him.

The sun warmed his back as he breathed deeply of the fresh air and sunshine. He loved Vargas Ranch and its craggy mountains with the expansive blue sky overhead. People who thought the desert was brown and boring missed the beauty of it. Golds, rusts, tans of the rocks, dirt, and mountains. Green scrub brush and palo verde trees. The dark brown rough bark of the mesquite trees contrasted with their little green leaves. Bright green saguaro cacti with their fat, spiny arms reaching toward heaven. In the summer, big white flowers with thick yellow pistils topped the crown. Since it was mid-December, the crown of the glorious cacti remained bare.

His favorite time of year was the spring. In years with heavy winter rains, the full color of the blooming desert came to life. Bright pink prickly pear cacti fruit. Yellow poppies grew from nowhere next to grass that covered the tan, almost white, dirt of the desert floor. Barrel cacti sported bright yellow fruit or flowers. In years with less winter rains, many cacti and other plants still bloomed, but the grass and yellow poppies might not.

In some ways, the desert reminded Dylan of life. Some years, so many exciting, wonderful things happened — like dating Brisa. Other years, life carried on, brief moments of beauty poking out between the rough patches — like Brisa's life earlier this year.

Last night, she had finally opened up in more detail about the abuse she suffered from Tristin. It hurt his heart to picture her trapped in the horrible relationship. She said God had rescued her through the accident. She just wished He hadn't taken Braden's legs in the process.

The high-pitched ringtone of Dylan's phone shattered the tranquil stillness, making his heart race. Struggling to rein in the crazed stallion, Dylan berated himself for forgetting to switch his phone to silent mode. The smell of horse sweat mixed with Thunder's fear, adding to the tension tightening his shoulders.

The deafening sound of Thunder's hooves echoed through the air, sending clouds of dust swirling. The majestic stallion danced and pranced, his mane whipping wildly in the wind. The ringing phone only agitated the horse further, causing him to rear up on his hind legs. Dylan struggled to maintain his balance, feeling the heaving of Thunder's sides with each breath. Despite his best efforts, the ringtone only grew louder, intensifying the chaos of the moment.

Blue sky and sunlight filled his vision as he soared through the air. His back landed hard on the unforgiving ground, stealing the breath from his lungs. His head ached as blackness swallowed him, accompanied by the fading bells of his phone.

BRISA'S PHONE VIBRATED in her back pocket as she eased the sheet over her client's back. She whispered the session ended and hurried from the room. She squinted under the bright hall lights as she grabbed her phone. The time read three on the dot.

She tapped her messages. One from Renata. *911. All experienced riders needed. Search & rescue. Dylan missing.*

Brisa's heart lodged in her throat. What happened? How long had he been gone? He told her last night he might miss their usual lunch date, but that was hours ago.

She texted Renata back as she walked to the lobby. "Jody, can you take Mrs. Avery cold water? Offer my apologies."

"Go. We've got things covered here."

Brisa jogged toward the barn. Adan rushed from the stables, mounting a palomino gelding. When he saw her, he hesitated.

"What happened?"

"He rode out on Thunder this morning. He should have been back hours ago."

Adan lifted his hat and ran a hand through his hair, expression grim.

Her phone buzzed again.

"That's the route he planned to take," Adan said as he dismounted. "You gonna ride with us?"

"Yeah."

"Take the horse Parker is saddling. I'll wait for you."

Brisa's pulse thrummed against her skin as perspiration dotted her back. Dylan, an experienced rider, had been missing for hours. A sob threatened to choke the air from her lungs. She swallowed it down as she entered the stable. She had to keep it together.

"Adan said I should take this horse," she told Parker.

He handed her the reins, and she hurried from the building. Her work uniform and comfy sneakers were terrible for riding, but it didn't matter. Dylan needed her. She would ride bareback if it meant finding him quicker.

As soon as Adan saw her, he dropped his hat on her head. Then he gave her a leg up before mounting his horse again.

"This way!"

He kicked the horse to a canter toward the north, and Brisa followed his lead. When the fence line came into view, he turned the horse toward the west. Already her legs burned, reminding her just how long it had been since she had ridden. It didn't matter. Dylan could be injured, and they had to find him.

Lord, please help us. I don't want to lose him.

The rest of the prayer died on her breath. She saw a cloud of dust from the south headed their direction. After a minute, the shape of cowboys and their horses came into focus. Derin. Devon.

"Just saw the message." Derin reined in beside them.

Adan's jaw twitched as he stopped his horse. Brisa angled hers next to theirs.

"He said he was going to ride the north perimeter, then head west toward Dalton Peak."

"When's the last time you heard from him?" Derin asked, a natural born leader.

"Nine-thirty."

"His horse come back?"

Adan shook his head. She knew enough about ranching and riding to know none of this was good. *Please, Lord, keep him safe. I love him.*

"Make sure your phones are on vibrate. Let's keep in touch with texts. You two look for him on the east side of Dalton Peak. We'll circle around to the back side."

Adan's sharp nod answered as he turned his horse toward Dalton Peak. Brisa followed.

When they slowed to a walk, she asked, "Do you know what he was wearing today?"

Adan snorted. "A checkered shirt and jeans? We haven't exactly been talking lately."

She wanted to remind him of his stupidity, but now was not the time.

"What color is his hat?"

"A yellow tan."

Adan's scowl deepened, and she turned away, scanning the ground for any sign of color, yellow or otherwise. Jeans would blend in with the shadows, but a plaid shirt and his hat should stick out. She hoped.

Even at a walk, her scrubs began chafing her thighs. She ignored the discomfort and pressed on.

Braden came to mind, and she slid her phone from her pocket. She texted Renata, assuming she had stayed behind. An all employee text relayed not to worry about the kids in childcare. Brisa breathed a little easier.

Then her eyes snagged on a yellow lump. "There!"

Adan's head snapped in the direction she pointed. He kicked his horse into a trot. When he neared the lump, Brisa held her breath. He dismounted and picked up the hat. He handed it to her, and she gave him his hat back before she donned Dylan's. She shoved away her fear when she realized Dylan wasn't close by.

"Looks like hoof prints. Text everyone our GPS location."

She typed out the message. Derin replied they would be

there in ten.

While Adan searched on foot, Brisa walked her horse, knowing the higher vantage point might help her spot something Adan couldn't see from the ground.

Then she saw it. Blood. Her stomach knotted as she shot another prayer heavenward.

"Adan over there!"

She watched him jog toward the dried blood, unwilling to follow. Fear constricted her throat. He could be dead. The emotions threatened to overwhelm her while the other riders converged on their location. As Adan approached, he shook his head.

"Found his phone. Looks like the horse trampled it." He held up the device with a shattered screen.

She saw his fear before he masked it. Even if he was being a stubborn idiot, he still cared about Dylan.

"No clear signs of which way he went."

She listened as Derin and Adan strategized. A few other men interjected ideas. Brisa's eyes blurred with unshed tears as she looked toward the eastern horizon.

Suddenly, a shadow moved in the distance. She blinked, and it stopped before disappearing. Had she seen something that wasn't there?

A bad feeling twisted her stomach. She kicked her horse into a trot in that direction, keeping her gaze locked onto the spot. Nothing became clear as her horse closed the gap.

Then something else caught her attention—light blue or white material. The pattern of his shirt became clearer as they neared. It was Dylan!

As soon as she reined in her horse, she dismounted and rushed to his side.

"Dylan!" She swallowed down a sob before it escaped.

He groaned as he sat up. Then he squinted against the light. His face paled, and he leaned onto his side, tossing up everything from his stomach. Brisa kneeled beside him and rubbed his back.

"Bri?" His voice sounded weak, and he had to be thirsty. Even though the temperatures were in the seventies, being out in the sun all day could dehydrate a person.

Her phone buzzed, and she read the message. She texted back that she found him. The thundering of horse hooves preceded a group of men and horses. Adan was at her side with some water.

"Sit up, Dyl," he said as he helped him, his voice gentle.

"I think he has a concussion," Brisa said. "He's dizzy and vomiting."

"Take a sip." Adan pressed a water bottle to Dylan's lips as his arm held him steady.

The purr of a UTV engine sounded in the distance as it stirred up a cloud of dust. The murmur of the men's voices faded as she wiped Dylan's brow with a dampened hand-kerchief.

A wry smile quirked his sunburned face. "You look good in my hat."

Brisa sucked in a deep breath—the first since learning he was missing. Then she expelled a light laugh as she set his hat on his head.

"Don't scare me like that again, wrangler."

His eyes closed as he leaned against Adan, the hint of a smile stretching his lips.

18

DYLAN SQUINTED AGAINST the bright sunlight, his head pounding like the loud bass from Adan's old stereo. He leaned his head against the seat back when the world started spinning.

"You okay?" Derin's voice sounded strained. "I can turn around."

"I'll be fine." No way he wanted to go back to the hospital. Tahoor, Dalton's ER doctor friend, said he might feel like a freight train hit him. Not exactly his words, but something like that.

"Maybe I should take you up to the house."

"No." The last thing he needed was Mami hovering over him all weekend. He needed to hear Brisa's voice before falling asleep until morning.

"I owe you an apology."

Dylan cracked one eye open and angled his head toward his arrogant, too-proud-for-his-own-good brother, who never apologized for anything.

"I've been dealing with... Some stuff." Derin groused as he ran a hand through his short, dark brown hair. "I shouldn't have taken it out on you. You know, when you went on your date last week."

Dylan opened the other eye. "What stuff?"

"Bro, I'm trying to apologize to you."

"Appreciate it. What stuff?"

Derin gripped the wheel so tight his knuckles paled. He ground his jaw. Dylan forced his eyes to stay open. He had always been good at silently waiting Derin out.

"I... Let's just say I have dated no one since May."

Dylan sat up straighter, fully awake despite the throbbing at the back of his head. He assumed Derin meant he hadn't slept with a woman either. No one ever talked about it, but everyone knew Derin hooked up with many single female guests during the peak season at the resort. Well, everyone except his parents. Maybe.

He considered his words. If Derin hadn't looked like he had spent the last day sleeping on cholla cacti, Dylan might have cracked a joke. Instead, he sent up a quick prayer for wisdom.

"Wanna talk about it?"

"No. Not with the family. I'm... I have someone I talk to. Regular like."

"Can I pray for you?"

Derin snorted. "I should pray for you, big brother. You're the one fresh out of the hospital. You scared us all."

It had scared Dylan, too.

"We can pray for each other, you know."

Derin coughed as he slowed his dually, turning down the gravel lane to the bunkhouse. His mouth opened and closed a few times.

"You can keep me in your prayers."

He sensed Derin didn't want a prayer in that moment, so he said, "Will do."

His younger brother remained quiet. He parked his truck and helped Dylan to his bunk. Before he flipped off the lights, he held Dylan's gaze for a good minute.

"Thanks for not dying out there today."

Dylan raised one side of his mouth. "Couldn't leave you with no one as a thorn in your side."

Derin belly laughed. "I think you got it backwards. Holler if you need anything."

"I wanted to. Now rest. I'll wake you went it's ready."

His sheepish smile stirred the butterflies in her stomach.

Brisa entered the kitchen and turned on the oven, allowing it to heat while she brought in everything. Then she placed the meatloaf and potatoes in the oven to bake. While it cooked, she prepared the brownies. As soon as the food finished, she set it on the counter and put the brownies in.

She found two plates and silverware. Then she carried them into the living room. The aroma of a home cooked meal must have woken him, because he flashed a lazy grin that warmed her from head to toe.

"Smells good."

Brisa handed him a plate. Then she grabbed two drinks from the kitchen before sitting next to him on the couch. He prayed for the meal and they ate.

"This is good," he said after a few bites. "Thank you."

"Mom always said comfort food could make a person heal twice as fast."

Dylan's chuckle made her smile.

"Dessert too?"

"Brownies. They'll be ready in a few minutes."

"Careful, you'll spoil me."

Brisa nudged him with her arm. "You could stand to be spoiled now and then."

"So could you."

She shrugged as she popped her last bite of meatloaf into her mouth.

"Not that I wouldn't have loved the horse ride, but this is nice, too. An afternoon with you."

He smiled. "I could do without the headache."

"Maybe fresh baked brownies will help."

She stood, and he handed her the plates.

"You can stretch out. I'll bring the brownies shortly."

After she loaded the dirty dishes into the dishwasher and placed the leftovers in the fridge, clearly marked with Dylan's name and a "hands off Adan", she portioned the brownies. Setting two on his plate, and one on hers, she joined him in the living room again.

His eyes were closed and his breathing shallow. She placed the brownies on the side table. She really wanted to sit next to him, letting his head rest in her lap. Stare at his day-old scruff. Rub her hand along his arm. But she couldn't figure how to do that without waking him. So she sat by his feet instead. When his arm flopped to the floor, his knuckles connected with the tile, jolting him awake.

"Sorry," he whispered as he slowly sat up.

"No worries. You need to rest."

He scooted down and patted the spot next to him. She moved to that side of the couch and handed him the brownies.

"Mmm. Still warm."

She smiled and watched him eat one. He handed her the second one back.

"For later. I'm tired."

Brisa set a throw pillow in her lap and he shimmied down on the couch until his head rested on it. His gorgeous chocolate eyes looked up at her. She ran her hand along his scruffy face. He looked good with a beard. Sexy. She released a stuttered breath at the thought.

He turned his face toward her hand and placed a kiss on it. Then his eyes fluttered closed.

What was happening to her? She had only been dating him for a week. Already she could glimpse a future with him in it. Always. Shouldn't it be too soon to feel so close to Dylan?

He was the best of men. Courageous. Kind. Loving. The complete opposite of her ex.

Brisa remembered what Dylan had told Braden the night of the hayride—that Jesus loved him no matter what. He would make an excellent father for her son.

She froze at the thought. Way too soon to think about something like that. Yet last night, he said he loved her. He must not think it was too soon.

When Dylan stirred, she shifted to rest her back against the arm of the couch, crossing her legs under the pillow under his head.

"Keep your eyes closed," she whispered.

"Hmm?"

Then she lightly placed her ring fingers on the pressure point of his jawline while rubbing her thumbs over his brow. Her index fingers moved in circles over his cheekbones as she continued the motion along his brow. Slowly, she worked her way up to his hairline, his dark, thick hair soft against her fingertips. She placed one hand under the back of his skull while working over his scalp with her index finger and thumb, avoiding where he hit his head. Once she reached the crown, she worked her way back down his face, then his sturdy neck and shoulders. Several times during the massage, he moaned softly, much like a baby's content cooing.

She ended the massage with light, sweeping movements down his arms. Then she leaned over him and pressed her lips against his forehead.

His eyes eased open as a blissful smile stretched across his lips. "Thank you."

The roughness in his voice sent a ripple of pleasure through her body. She was definitely falling for this shy cowboy.

DYLAN'S HEADACHE FADED under Brisa's soothing touch. She was so good to him. Bringing him food. Spending the afternoon with him, even though he slept through most of it. The face massage. It felt unbelievably good and totally platonic until she ended it with her soft lips against his forehead.

He cleared his throat and opened his eyes to her upside-down face. Her sky-blue eyes gazed upon him, full of love. She might not be ready to say the words yet, but her eyes told him everything. When her gaze flicked away, pink colored her cheeks.

Dylan eased himself upright, gripping the back of the couch when a wave of dizziness washed over him. He groaned. Brisa's palm flattened between his shoulder blades.

"Are you okay?"

"Dizzy."

"Given your concussion, it's not surprising. Go slow."

She left her hand against his back as he swung his legs over the edge of the couch.

"Maybe I should go to bed."

Her hand rubbed circles in the center of his back. Then her arm wrapped around his waist. "Let me help you."

He slung his arm over her shoulders and stood. When he swayed, her arm tightened around him. Her other hand shot to his hip.

"Easy."

They shuffled with small steps to his bunk, taking what felt like an hour to get there. Once he reclined on his bed, she placed a hand on his shoulder.

"Do you need anything else?"

He shook his head, and nausea rolled over him. Squeezing his eyes shut and locking his jaw, he willed the bile to stay where it belonged. He blew out a slow breath as the sensation passed.

"Let me bring you some water."

When she turned to leave, he caught her arm. "I'll be fine. Thanks for lunch. Sorry, I'm not good company today."

Brisa turned back toward him, her fingers combing his hair off his face. Then she leaned over and pressed her lips to his, her hand resting over his heart. He froze as longing for her overwhelmed him. Her face hovered over his, mere inches separating them. All he had to do was place his hand on her neck and draw her close again. He could part his lips and allow her kisses.

Instead, his hand found the one warming his chest. He squeezed it.

"Thanks for everything."

She straightened slowly, a shy smile on her lips, admiration shining in her eyes. "Sweet dreams, Dylan."

His last thought as she walked away brought a smile to his face. Sometimes not kissing was more heated than kissing. Or so he guessed, as he had yet to give her an actual kiss.

19

SUNDAY MORNING, DYLAN woke feeling well rested. Adan and Parker had fed the horses, allowing him to sleep in. As the sound of banter and showers floated down the hall, he eased out of bed. No dizziness this time.

His movements felt sluggish as he shaved, showered, and dressed for church.

"You can ride with me, bro," Derin said as he shoved his feet into his boots.

Yeah, that was probably smarter than driving himself while not feeling back to normal yet. He climbed into his brother's dually, fastened his seat belt, and closed his eyes.

"You want to hang back today?"

"No. Mami won't like that."

Derin chuckled. They both knew she had exhibited unusual restraint by not showing up at the bunkhouse to take care of him. Maybe someone told her Brisa had come by yesterday.

When they arrived, Brisa found him, a bright smile on her face. She wrapped her arms around him as he placed a kiss on her cheek.

"You look better today."

"Still a little out of sorts. And tired."

"Do you feel up to dinner at my parents' house?"

"If you don't mind driving."

"Of course."

Her arms released him and she squeezed his hand before she took her place with her family. He sat in his usual seat in his family's row. Hopefully Mami wouldn't mind him skipping family dinner.

The worship service brought a healing peace to his soul, and he found the pastor's message challenging. But he felt guilty as he eagerly strode over to Brisa after service, like he could have paid more attention.

He rode with her to her parents' house, a place he had visited often as a teen. Even as an adult when Adan lived there, he had regularly hung out in their home. Now he was there for Brisa and Braden.

A smile stretched across his face as she parked along the street in front of the two story stucco house. Painted a light tan, which complemented the teal accents on the door and pop outs around the large windows. A large cottonwood tree shaded the front yard. A wide porch ran the length of the house, flush with the edge of the concrete driveway. The double garage door, painted a cream color, still held the dent from that time Adan accidentally backed his dad's truck into it. Harley had chuckled when it happened, using the situation as a life lesson. Heidi had been less than pleased until Harley told her it gave their curb appeal some character.

Harley greeted them at the door, swinging it wide open. Dylan's eyes glanced at the living room. Same furniture, decor, and arrangement as the last time he had visited. Something about the lack of changes comforted him. Harley and Heidi both greeted him with hugs before showing him to the dining room table. Braden asked to sit beside him, so Brisa made space between them. He would have enjoyed Brisa sitting right next to him, but getting to know Braden better was a good thing.

After Harley prayed over the meal, Heidi passed a platter of fried chicken to Dylan, treating him like an honored guest instead of an old family friend. He wasn't sure why it stood out to him, but it did. The metal tongs clinked against the china when he rested them against it. He held the platter for Brisa and she chose a large chicken breast, placing it on her plate.

"I'll cut up some of mine for Braden."

Dylan handed the platter to Harley before dishing up potatoes for himself and Braden. He swirled gravy over both mounds of potatoes before handing it off to Brisa. She glanced up through her long lashes with a soft smile on her lips before returning her attention to portioning chicken bites for her son. His breath caught. She truly was a wonderful mother. It suited her and, for a moment, he could see another little boy with dark hair and brown eyes sitting next to her.

Harley's voice stirred him from the pleasant vision. "Brisa tells us you're managing the stables now."

"Yes, sir."

Harley laughed. "I think you're plenty old enough to call me Harley, don't you?"

Dylan's face warmed, and he nodded sharply.

"Harley." The name felt odd on his tongue. This man was Papi's best friend. Adan and Brisa's father. It seemed strange to speak to him man to man.

"Papi mentioned you left your job for the city," Dylan said.

"Yeah, a buddy of mine was looking for an estimator with a civil engineering background. The salary makes up for the benefits I lost from the city. I can work from home a few days a week, too."

"Which I love," Heidi said with a big smile. "I make lunch for us both. Or sometimes we go out to Greta's café, The Lariat."

"We're calling it my pre-retirement job." Harley chuckled.

"Mom, I forgot to ask. Can you take Braden to physical therapy on Monday?" Brisa asked.

"I've told you before, I can always take him. Monday,

Wednesday, and Friday."

Dylan angled toward Brisa. Her lips pursed in a tight line, and he wondered why she refused the offer.

"He's my responsibility."

"And I don't work, honey. I'm more than happy to spend the time with my darling grandson."

"I enjoy going with Grandma," Braden said. "Sometimes she takes me for ice cream after."

"See?" Heidi's eyebrow rose.

Brisa's shoulders sagged. "Thank you, Mom. I appreciate it."

"And you'll let me take him all three days per week?"

Dylan watched his girlfriend. Her eyes reddened and darted to the corner of the room as she slowly nodded her head. He knew she felt guilty about her son's disability. Perhaps her reluctance came from some misplaced sense that it was her punishment for not leaving her ex. He reached over and placed his hand at the base of her neck, rubbing his thumb along the tense muscle. When a tear escaped and trailed down her cheek, he wiped it away. She offered him a wan smile. Oh, how he wished he could carry some of her burden for her.

"More chicken," Braden said.

"What do you say?" Brisa chided.

"Please."

"Here, have some of mine." Dylan cut off a chunk and cut it up before scraping it onto Braden's plate.

"Thanks!"

When they finished eating, Brisa stood and started clearing plates. Dylan took the stack from her.

"I'll help. Why don't you go play with Braden?" he suggested.

"But you're our guest."

He gave her a look that he hoped conveyed what he thought about that.

"Fine. Thank you."

Harley shooed Heidi away as well. Dylan started putting leftovers in plastic containers, which were in the same place as always.

Harley snorted as Dylan stacked them in the fridge. "I forget how well you know our family and our house."

"I remember the rule," Dylan said. "The ladies cook for us. We tackle the dishes."

"Tres and Catalina raised you well."

Dylan's chest puffed out just a little under the praise.

"When she's ready, you have my blessing."

Dylan's throat went dry when he realized exactly what Harley meant. "We only started dating, sir."

Harley raised his eyebrow.

"Harley."

"That's better. Whether Bri has pieced it together yet or not, I don't know. But the rest of us can see plain as day that you've loved her for a long time. I'd venture a guess that no other woman would ever be right for you."

Dylan swallowed down the lump in his throat. "I l-l-love her with my entire s-s-soul."

Harley clamped a hand down on his shoulder and squeezed. "Heidi and I are praying for the three of you."

"Thank you, s—, Harley."

The older man grinned, reminding him of Brisa's infectious smile.

"Now go have fun with her and Braden. I'm sure he'd love to share his legos with you."

Dylan smiled and headed to the living room, in awe of the Franco's perceptiveness and acceptance. Now he and Adan needed to patch things up.

BRISA FLATTENED AGAINST the dining room wall, just out of sight when she realized Dad and Dylan were talking about her. She intended to refill her water, but Dad's words stopped her in her tracks.

"When she's ready, you have my blessing."

Had Dylan asked for her hand already? Even after all the horrible things about herself that she had confessed to him? Her heart rammed against her chest as she tried to breathe quieter.

"We only started dating."

Dad's voice softened. Something about Dylan loving her for a long time? That wasn't possible. He had been so distant in high school. Then she moved away and had been gone for a decade.

"I l-l-love her with my entire s-s-soul."

Tears burned the back of her eyes. She sniffed and set her cup on the dining room table before running up the stairs to her childhood room. She flopped down on her old bed, muffling her sobs with her pillow. Dylan shouldn't waste such love on her. She didn't deserve love like that. He was too good for her.

Wasn't that just like life? Tristin treated her like dirt. Dylan put her on a pedestal. Two stark extremes. Neither healthy.

A soft knock sounded on her door before the hinges creaked open.

"Bri?" Mom's voice revealed her concern. "What is it, honey?"

The bed sank a little to her right as her mom sat next to her. Gentle circles on her back soothed her, like Mom's care always had.

"He... Loves me... With his entire soul."

"Hmm. He does. Has for some time. Always will, I have no doubt."

"Mom, no one can love like that."

Brisa pushed up and sat cross-legged, hugging her soaked pillow tightly against her chest.

"No one?" Mom's eyebrow arched high. "Not even Jesus? Or a man fully surrendered to him?"

Brisa frowned and looked down at her hands, afraid to allow the truth of Mom's words to wrap around her heart. Tristin's accusations tried to fight for her attention. She was worthless. A terrible mother. Selfish for wanting a little time for herself. She didn't deserve love.

Lies. She knew they were lies. Her counselor reminded her of it during every session. When would she believe it, though? Could she?

"Do you trust Dylan?"

Brisa's eyes snapped up to her mother's. She knew the right answer, but it wouldn't make it past her lips. Probably a good sign that she still didn't quite believe he was real.

Mom rested her hand over Brisa's. "It will come in time. He is a patient man. He'll give you the space you need."

Brisa snorted. "He hasn't even kissed me yet."

Mom's eyes widened as her eyebrows shot heavenward. "Really?"

A smile flitted around the corner of Brisa's mouth. "He knows I want him to. But he holds back, even though I can see it in his eyes. He wants to kiss me."

"But he knows you're not ready yet. And that's why your father and I trust him completely. His character is impeccable. His faith is strong. And, as you overheard, he loves you completely. Deeply."

Brisa's shoulders rose as she filled her lungs with a deep breath. She released it slowly as she tossed her pillow aside and swiped her fingers over her damp cheeks.

"Thanks, Mom."

Mom held her arms wide, and Brisa leaned into her comforting embrace. After a few seconds, Mom released her and stood.

"Come on down when you're ready."

Brisa nodded before her mother closed the door behind her, the latch softly clicking into place. She stood and checked her appearance in the mirror. No way to hide that she had been crying. She cleaned up the mascara smudges, straightened her shoulders, and padded down the stairs.

Before her feet hit the bottom step, she looked up. Braden sat with his back against Dylan's chest. Dylan reclined on the floor behind him, propped on one elbow. The other arm suspended in the air around her son, holding a bright yellow lego brick. Braden's neck craned around to look at Dylan's face, hanging on his words. Dylan whispered something to her son, and Braden giggled. Then he accepted the block and snapped it into place.

"Like this?"

Dylan whispered something to Braden, and his joyous giggles echoed in the room. Brisa's breath caught. She could picture a little boy with dark hair and chocolate eyes hanging on Dylan's back. A little girl with blond pigtails in a pink dress sitting nearby smiling up at her daddy.

A father for her son. Isn't that what she had prayed for when she posted her profile online?

The bottom stair moaned as she stepped onto it. Dylan's dreamy chocolate eyes traveled up her bare feet, jeans, blouse, and finally locked with hers. A grin spread across his face, almost as if he read her thoughts. This connection he had with her was special. He was special.

Heat warmed her cheeks as she crossed the room, their eyes never breaking contact. She eased onto the mat on the floor across from Dylan and her son. At last, she broke their gaze when her eyes flicked to Braden.

"Mommy, look what we're building!"

Braden's smile always had a cathartic effect on whatever trouble brewed in her heart. Now was no different.

"A stable. For horses."

"Oh?"

"Dylan said we need this," he pointed to an opening in the blocks, "so they can get out."

"I see."

"Mommy?"

"Yes, baby?"

"Can I get some horses?"

Brisa's throat constricted as her eyes darted to Dylan. He didn't promise something she couldn't deliver, did he? She hated breaking her son's heart.

"He means lego horses." Dylan's deep voice soothed her fear.

"I'll see what I can find online."

Braden pushed up, standing on his stumps. Wait! He was standing! Her breath left in a whoosh as he took two steps toward her before launching into her arms. When did he learn how to do that?

"Love you, Mommy."

She blinked back her tears. "Love you too, Braden." She craned her neck to her mother, raising an eyebrow in question. Mom shrugged.

No matter how it happened, Brisa was grateful for the small milestone in her son's development. One more step, literally, toward an independent future.

Dylan yawned, reminding Brisa that he still suffered the aftereffects of a concussion. She ought to drive him home. She started to stand, but Dylan shook his head.

"Derin will be here in a few minutes. I didn't want to pull you away from time with your son."

Yeah, she wasn't sure when it happened, when she had moved from the falling-for-him to loving him. But love him, she did.

The doorbell rang, and Dad answered it. Dylan sat upright and scooted closer to her before placing a hand on her neck, drawing her head close to his. His lips veered to her forehead, pressing a warm kiss there before he released her.

"Call me tonight?" he whispered.

She loved their evening calls. They learned so much about each other during those times and she wouldn't miss the opportunity. She nodded before he stood and left with his brother.

Yeah, Dylan Vargas had stolen her heart when she wasn't looking. And she would be happy to let him keep it.

20

DYLAN RAN A hand through his hair as he set his hat on its hook inside of his office. He had a dozen things to wrap up by the end of the day — the day before he would propose to Brisa. He sat down in his office chair and powered on his laptop, leg bobbing up and down while he waited.

Popping the lid off the coffee drink Drake handed him after breakfast, he sniffed it. The scent of peppermint and chocolate drifted up to his nose. He eyed it before taking a sip. Not bad. He had never been one to order fancy coffee drinks, but this might change his mind. Now he understood why Drake's coffee bar was always so busy.

When his laptop screen finally flickered on, he opened his email. Shannon mentioned sending him a few links about service dogs for amputee children. She found one place that had a dog for a young child, but it ended up not being a good match. That bit of news gave him a reality check. Finding the right dog wasn't as simple as ordering one online and paying the money. The animal needed to bond with its owner and vice versa. Sometimes dogs trained for over a year and washed out of the program. All those broken hearts. He prayed this dog would be the one for Braden. If not, it was in danger of flunking and being adopted as a pet instead of a service dog.

He punched the phone number into his phone and waited for a few rings. A woman named Caitlin answered after the third ring. She had been expecting his call. Dylan shared more details about Braden's situation. He spent the last two weeks peppering Brisa with questions to learn absolutely everything about his future son. Or so he hoped. So, he could answer all of Caitlin's questions.

By the time the call ended, they agreed Dylan, Brisa, and Braden could fly up to Wisconsin at the end of January to meet the standard poodle named Scout. If she was a suitable match for Braden, they wouldn't be bringing her home yet. Scout would have another three to six months of training to complete with adjustments for Braden's specific needs. They could visit Scout a few times during those months.

"Hey, boss." Adan's cold greeting stabbed Dylan's heart. "You asked to see me."

Despite his diligent prayers, Adan still hadn't forgiven him. At least most days, they were amiable at work.

"Have a seat."

A frown flicked over Adan's features. Not surprising. Rarely did Dylan have so much to talk to him about that he offered a seat, knowing Adan preferred to stand and get back to work quickly.

"You still want to go in on the charity?" Dylan asked.

Adan's stiff posture melted, and he rubbed a hand on the back of his neck. "Yeah."

"I was thinking we should call it Braden's Hope."

Adan held his gaze as his eyes glistened. Dylan had seen a lot of emotions from his best friend, but this was new. Adan coughed as he broke eye contact.

"I owe you an apology."

Please, Lord, let him forgive me.

"After a lot of soul searching, and a swift kick in my behind from my sister and my nephew, I realized I completely overreacted." Adan's blue eyes locked on his. "I was hurt, Dyl, that you hid it. That was the only part of my reaction that had anything to do with you. The rest of it?"

Adan cleared his throat as he turned his attention to the

painting on the wall above the couch.

"I'm her big brother. I'm supposed to protect her." His voice cracked and his throat worked. "I was off bull riding, making a name for myself while my little sister was trapped with that…"

Dylan understood the feeling. Knowing everything Brisa suffered at her ex's hands was difficult to come to terms with it. He should have realized how much harder it would be for Adan as her brother.

"Three time World Champion means nothing — not now, knowing I failed Brisa."

"You didn't know." Because if he had, Dylan knew Adan would have moved heaven and earth to rescue his sister.

Adan propped his elbows on his knees and dropped his head in his hands. Dylan could sense he struggled for control, though if his friend broke down, it might be good for him.

When Adan lifted his head, Dylan noticed the tears pooling in his eyes.

"The worst part is that I can't do anything now. The guy is dead. No way to extract my two pounds of flesh. I can't give him a piece of my mind. I failed to protect her and there's nothing I can do to make it right."

Dylan let out a loud breath. "God protected her, Adan. He rescued her. It wasn't your destiny, nor mine, to save her. God had a plan and a purpose as hard as that is to swallow. And believe me, it's hard."

Dylan stood and rounded his desk. He leaned against the front and squeezed Adan's shoulder.

"But now He's inviting you and me into a few things. First, He's given us Braden's Hope as a way to bring hope to other children, men, and women who have lost limbs. There are so many in need and so many ways to meet those needs — if someone pays for it all. That's where we come in. Where Braden's Hope makes a difference."

Dylan dropped his hand and crossed his arms over his chest.

"Second, God has invited us to be there for both Brisa and Braden now. Me, hopefully as her husband and Braden's dad, if she says yes tomorrow. You get to be the doting uncle and trustworthy brother. After those few years of suffering, Brisa gets two men to stand guard for her now."

Adan coughed. He wiped his eyes on his sleeve.

"And God has invited us to be family. The Francos—you—have always been as much of our family mission as any blood-born Vargas. We, you and me, do not deviate from the Lord's plan."

Dylan kicked Adan's booted foot.

"So what do you say, brother? Will you turn all that guilt into motivation to make a difference in others' lives with me?"

Adan nodded. "Yeah. Yeah, I will."

"Good, now bring it in."

Adan stood and Dylan gave him a man hug, knowing he had his best friend's forgiveness.

"So, you're popping the question tomorrow, huh?"

"Wish me luck."

Adan laughed. "No luck needed. She's gonna say yes."

"Hello?" Padre's gravelly voice came from the doorway.

Adan mumbled an excuse and hurried from Dylan's office as Papi and Padre entered.

"What brings you both here? I would have come over to the ranch house if you'd asked."

"Padre wanted out of the house," Papi said.

"Your mami and River are baking Christmas cookies for the staff and it's too tempting to sit around smelling all that." Padre's mischievous smile revealed Mami had probably booted him out for stealing too many cookies.

Dylan chuckled. "Come on in."

Papi sat in the chair Adan had vacated. Padre shuffled toward Dylan, digging in his pocket.

174

"I know I'm probably late giving this to you."

He held out a simple gold ring with a round cut diamond in the center flanked by two smaller ones.

"It was my mother's ring."

Great-grandma Maria — the true matriarch. The woman who picked out this piece of land and convinced Great-grandpa Dalton to buy it when Padre was Braden's age. The significance was not lost on Dylan.

"Dalton, as the firstborn, gets the ranch house and a few other perks. But I've been saving this for one of you boys. When I saw you with Brisa and Braden, I knew I had been saving it for you."

Dylan accepted the ring, setting it on his desk. Then he pulled Padre into a big hug before escorting him to the chair next to Papi.

"You know, I've been shopping three times for the perfect ring and haven't been able to find it. I was gonna try again this afternoon."

"So you didn't buy one yet?" Papi asked. "That's cutting it close."

"Or God's provision," Padre said, patting Papi's hand.

"I'm honored, Padre, to offer Great-grandma's ring to the woman I love."

"Good. Now, Tres, tell him your news."

Papi cleared his throat. "Your mami and I have set aside four parcels of land, one for each of you boys other than Dalton, since he owns the ranch house now."

Dylan blinked. "Land?"

"For a house, son. I know Brisa only moved into her house a month ago, so we'll understand if you decide you don't want to build right away. But," Papi said, pulling a piece of paper from his back pocket, "It's yours. Do with it what you want, when you want."

Dylan unfolded the paper. Five acres. Plenty of space for a house. Or houses — for Braden and his future children. The map included with the deed showed it was next to the ranch house property line to the south.

He stood and hugged his papi, humbled by the gift. He would let Brisa decide when they should build because he would be content to live in her house as long as she wanted to.

"Thank you both. For everything."

"I'm proud of you, son."

The words meant the world to him.

Then Papi and Padre prayed with him for tomorrow and for his future with Brisa and Braden. They ended the prayer together.

"We do not deviate from Your plan."

BRISA ALLOWED DYLAN to give her a leg up on Frappe's back. She straightened her hat while he mounted his horse, Red. She breathed deeply of the crisp morning air.

With it being two days before Christmas, the meaning of the season wrapped around her heart. Her life had transformed in the last two and a half months since she moved home. Her faith had grown stronger as she learned to rely on God to tackle the impossible—helping her live like she believed in His love and Christ's sacrifice for her. Through that process, she trusted Him more than ever.

As they rode toward Dalton Peak, Brisa thanked God for so many things. For Braden's new outlook with the blades to help him walk and riding lessons he loved so much. For Dylan and his unbelievable love. She thanked God that He brought her a man full of integrity, one fully surrendered to his Savior. One that she felt safe with.

God had been good to her. He rescued her through that accident nearly a year ago. He brought her home where she belonged and thrived.

Now she eagerly looked forward to the next chapter of

her life, no longer looking back.

"Adan and I cleared the air." Dylan's voice cut through the still morning next to her.

The soft thuds of the horses' hooves mixed with the squeak of leather. The sun warmed her back, taking the edge off the chill as she breathed deeply of the smell of horse and desert.

"I'm glad he came to his senses."

"Turns out, he wasn't really mad at me. He just felt guilty for not being there for you."

"Yeah, he stopped by yesterday after work. We talked for hours."

"Good."

They fell into silence for several minutes—that sweet silence of two hearts entwined, content to be in each other's presence. Dylan would probably always be a man of fewer words than some. Brisa didn't mind. His actions had always spoken volumes. She knew he loved her and Braden.

After an hour, Dylan reined in his horse.

"This spot okay?" he asked.

"For what?"

"Our p-p-picnic lunch."

"Sure."

As she dismounted, she wondered why he was nervous, his stutter a clear sign of it. She tied Frappe to a low mesquite tree near Red while Dylan laid out a blanket and set out the food and water.

When she neared the blanket, he held her hands. The look he gave her sent her pulse spiking.

"Brisa Franco, I thought I loved you for a decade. But when you moved back, and I got to know the real you, I realized I did not know what love meant. You've turned my world upside down and shown me the true meaning of love."

He dropped to one knee, still holding her left hand. After rooting around in his jeans pocket, he held up a simple gold diamond ring.

Oh! This was happening now!

"I know it might seem soon, but I love you with all my heart and I don't want to live another day without you and Braden. Will you marry me? Will you let me adopt Braden as my son?"

Tears burned her eyes. He wanted Braden to be his son? It shouldn't surprise her. That's who Dylan was.

"Yes! Yes, I'll be your wife. And yes, of course you can adopt Braden."

Dylan slid the gold ring onto her finger. He cleared his throat as he stood.

"Um, sorry, it's a little loose. We can get it sized after Christmas."

His hands settled on her waist and she slid her arms up his chest until her wrists crossed behind his neck.

"Does this mean—"

He cut off her words as his lips moved across hers for their first kiss. A kiss she knew meant he loved her as much as he claimed. She felt his love in the tender melding of their lips. When his hand cupped her cheek, she pressed closer, longing for the day she would become his wife.

Slowly, he pulled back enough to rest his forehead against hers. His breath came in ragged gasps.

"Some first kiss, wrangler," she teased.

A smile tilted one side of his mouth. "Worth the wait?"

"Mmm. Yes. You and the kiss were worth the wait."

Dylan ran his hands down her arms and took a step back. "I love you, Brisa."

"I love you, too."

He held her hand, and she eased onto the blanket.

"One more question, my love."

"Yeah?"

"How do you feel about a New Year's Day wedding?"

Her eyes went wide. "As in nine days from now?"

"Sounds so far away."

Brisa laughed. "Alright. Since you asked nicely. New Year's Day it is. Now, kiss me again."

Her shy cowboy kissed her until she forgot all about lunch and quick weddings. She loved him with her entire soul, too.

Epilogue

DERIN FELT THE emotion bubble up in his chest as he watched his almost-sister-in-law stroll up the aisle of the cowboy church, her son Braden holding his mother's arm while he balanced on his blades hidden beneath dress slacks. Derin's were the only dry eyes in the room, and he wasn't certain they would stay dry. Adan coughed next to him, a sure sign he was getting choked up.

That little boy had to be one of the luckiest on the planet because today he was gaining a dad and four more uncles—three of which were good men.

Derin held back a snort. Last thing he wanted was to ruin Dylan's wedding day with his brooding.

They say—he did not know who "they" were, but whatever—they say every large family has at least one bad apple. Derin didn't have to look much further than a mirror to figure out who it was in his family.

Dalton, the firstborn, had always lived up to his strong moral compass. His closest brush with failure was with his ex-fiancée, Janessa. Yeah, that. If Dalton only knew what Derin did about her, he would have dumped her much sooner. When Dalton met River, Derin had been happy for him. They seemed great together.

Then there was Dylan. A saint if there ever was one. Again, Derin stifled a snort. Dylan hadn't even kissed his fiancée until after he proposed to her. Yeah, who did that?

181

Not Derin. He started kissing girls by fourteen. And more by sixteen. Who was the bad apple? Yeah, him. Hands down.

Devon wasn't as saintly as Dylan, but he came in as a close second. Then the baby, Drake, was — how had he heard him described? Oh, yeah. Hipster cowboy. Tats up both arms and who knew where else. Yet he dressed like a cowboy. Owned two motorcycles — the loud, manly kind. And a truck, because no self-respecting man could wear the label cowboy and own a Tesla or Prius. Honestly, Drake probably hadn't done more than kiss a girl. His bad-boy image was just a mask to compensate for being a mamacita's boy. And Derin, being good at three things, called him out on it from time to time.

Those three things Derin was good at? Leading men, making people angry, and hiding his sins.

Well, all that was changing. Starting tomorrow, he wouldn't be the foreman of Vargas Ranch anymore. He was starting his job as the manager, okay Dalton called him CEO, over the sports complex and rehab center. Program. Whatever. Dalton always did like long, complicated titles. It meant Derin had a ton to learn and would probably spend most of his days indoors. An enormous change from the first twenty-nine years of his life.

Devon tapped the back of his dress shoes — yuck — with his foot, Derin's signal to turn toward the bride and groom. Envy reared its ugly head. He wanted that. True love. A wife and family. Only he was the bad apple and bad apples never experienced a happily-ever-after.

But he was changing. Seeing a counselor since May. He knew deep down, if he wanted the white picket fence and two point five kids, he had to become a better man. He had to change his ways. Stop hiding his sins and confront them head on.

Derin was trying to do just that. Between one-on-one counseling weekly and group therapy at a church in Wickenburg every Thursday night, he was making strides. He hadn't been with a woman since May. That was hard-won progress.

And now that Cole Gregory worked for him, he would have the accountability he needed in his backyard without spilling his guts to his brothers or the rest of his family.

Derin and Cole first met when Cole stayed at the re-sort—it was how Derin met anyone. Cole was a sports agent, well-connected in tennis, baseball, and football circles. Cole had been looking for the real cowboy experience, and Derin drew the short-straw that day. It ended up being one of the best things in his life. They became fast friends, keeping in touch via FaceTime and text messages for the past six years. When Cole had downtime, which wasn't often, he came to the ranch. Best part, Cole was a strong Christian—a positive influence—without being overly pious or annoying like Dalton or Dylan.

Devon kicked his foot again, drawing Derin's attention back to the wedding. Dylan had just finished kissing his now wife. Good for him. Seriously, Derin was happy for his older brother, turned instant family man. It was a role he would excel at. Derin had no doubts. Again, saint.

Maybe one day Derin would conquer his demons and find a soulmate. Pigs could fly, right?

Read Derin's story in *Falling for a Bossy Cowboy (Vargas Ranch Book 3).*

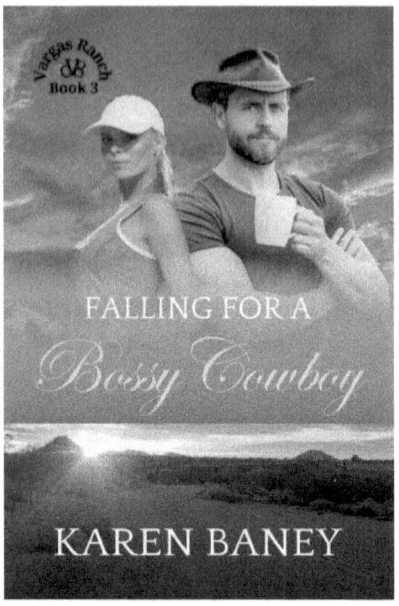

From the Author

So, when you create characters, you're not supposed to have favorites, right? If so, I might be in trouble, because Dylan is one of my favorites. I love how he learned to get past his stuttering long enough to woo Brisa. And I love he didn't quite realize the in-person version of himself was just as wonderful as Wrangler92.

I know some readers might not like that Brisa came from an abusive situation. I really wanted to show that she wasn't a victim, destined to fall for another toxic man. Instead, she fell for someone completely the opposite. She grew to trust God more and allow him to heal her brokenness.

You may ask, why make Braden disabled? I learned about a wonderful charity in Chino Valley that uses equine therapy to help disabled people and even those struggling with PTSD. Ever since then, I've wanted to incorporate equine therapy into one of my stories. Braden's character and his disability provided the opportunity, along with adding angst and joy.

I hope you enjoyed Dylan and Brisa's love match and the way Dylan instantly connected with Braden.

Look for Derin's story in *Falling for a Bossy Cowboy (Vargas Ranch Book 3)*. He gives up his position as the foreman of the ranch to start Vargas Sports with his friend. When he's drawn to the rehabbing tennis pro he wants to change from his bad boy ways. Will he be successful?

Karen Baney

About the Author

Karen Baney is passionate about writing stories full of flawed characters. She enjoys weaving together stories of second chances, redemption, and overcoming personal trials. As a transplant to Arizona, she loves researching the state's history and finding ways to seamlessly incorporate real history and real settings into her novels. In addition to writing and speaking, Karen works as a Software Development Manager for a Christian ministry.

Her faith plays an important role both in her life and in her writing. Karen and her husband, Jim, make their home in Gilbert, Arizona, with their two dogs, Bella and Daisy. Both Jim and Karen are active at Rock Point Church in Queen Creek, Arizona.

Discover faith-laced stories with characters who feel like lifelong friends.

Visit www.karenbaney.com to discover more historical romance series set in the American West. Follow Karen's writing journey and get behind-the-scenes glimpses of her research adventures on social media.

Facebook: @AuthorKarenBaney
X: @karen_baney
Instagram: @AuthorKarenBaney
BookBub: Follow Karen Baney for new release alerts

Books By Karen Baney

<u>Contemporary Romance</u>

Vargas Ranch Series:
Love is in the air at the Vargas Guest Ranch & Resort near Wickenburg, Arizona. Meet the Vargas family — five swoon-worthy brothers and their cousins who live by their family motto: "We do not deviate from the Lord's plan." These rugged cowboys run a successful working ranch and luxury resort while navigating the rollercoaster of finding true love.

Falling for a Fake Cowboy
Falling for a Real Cowboy
Honeymoon with a Real Cowboy
Falling for a Shy Cowboy
Falling for a Bossy Cowboy
Falling for a Smart Cowboy
Falling for a Humbug Cowboy
Falling for a Devoted Cowgirl
Falling for a Pregnant Cowgirl
Falling for a Cowboy's Legacy

Steadfast Love Series:
The *Steadfast Love* series follows a close-knit group of friends as they navigate the beautiful mess of modern life in the Phoenix area — workplace drama, complicated families, and love that shows up when they least expect it. These contemporary romances blend emotional depth with authentic faith, reminding us that even when life unravels, God's love never does.

The Heart I Rescue (prequel)
The Air I Breathe

Historical Western Romance

Prescott Pioneers Series:
Step back in time to the wild, untamed Arizona Territory where survival depends on grit, faith, and the courage to start over. Follow three pioneer families—the Andersons, Colters, and Larsons—as they risk everything for the promise of a new life in a land that demands both strength and hope.

A Dream Unfolding
A Heart Renewed
A Life Restored
A Hope Revealed
Hidden Prospects

Desert Manna Series:
Sometimes the most beautiful love stories bloom in the desert. Set in the growing frontier town of Prescott during the early 1870s, these tender romances follow women rebuilding their lives after heartbreak and the unexpected men who help them discover that second chances at love are worth the risk. Set in Prescott, Arizona between 1871 - 1873.

Beauty for Ashes
Joy for Mourning
Oaks of Justice

Colter Sons Series:
Power, legacy, and forbidden love collide in this sweeping family saga set in the Arizona Territory. The Colter ranch empire has weathered decades of frontier life, but now family secrets and buried betrayals threaten to destroy everything. As five brothers—and one resilient sister—navigate the treacherous waters of love, loss, and redemption, they must decide what's worth fighting for. Set in Prescott and

other locations within the Arizona Territory in 1887 - 1906.

The Reluctant Cattleman
The Roaming Adventurer
The Railroad Magnate
The Resourceful Stockman
The Restless Wrangler
The Resilient Bride

Larson Sisters Series
Meet the next generation! These delightful novellas follow the three daughters of Adam and Julia Larson from the *Prescott Pioneers Series* as they navigate love, courtship, and finding their own happily ever afters in territorial Arizona in 1886 – 1894.

In Love at Christmas
In Love with the Rancher
In Love with the Horse Trainer

Desert Life Media

Desert Life Media: *There Is Life in The Desert*

Entertainment-first Christian fiction set in the Southwest, featuring redemption, family, and faith

Publishing clean, wholesome, and uplifting fiction since 2010

desertlifemedia.com